June Masters Bacher

Love Is a Gentle Stranger

Sweet River Press®

Eugene, Oregon 97402

This is a work of fiction. Names, characters, places, and incidents are products of the author's imagination or are used fictitiously. Any resemblance to actual persons, living or dead, or to events or locales, is entirely coincidental.

Scripture quotations are taken from the King James Version of the Bible.

Cover by Katie Brady Design & Illustration, Eugene, Oregon

Cover photo © iStockphoto.com

LOVE IS A GENTLE STRANGER
Copyright © 1983 by George Bacher
Published by Sweet River Press®
Eugene, Oregon 97402

ISBN 978-1-59681-009-9

Printed in the United States of America

09 10 11 12 13 14 15 16 17 / DP-SK / 11 10 9 8 7 6 5 4 3 2 1

Relentless as the restless tides
That cast their burdens on the sand,
They come by ones, by twos, by hundreds,
Their keys of courage opening portals
Of the river's mountain lock,
Tilling, toiling, forcing nature
To bring forth fruit from stubborn acres,
Building homes and clearing land,
Moulding birthrights for their children...

—From *Umpqua Cavalcade*
By June Masters Bacher
Copyright © 1952

Dedicated to those valiant pioneers who unknowingly helped to write this book!

With special appreciation to Dr. Horace Robinson (director of *UMPQUA CAVALCADE),* Dr. Gordon Howard (assistant director), Henry Barneck (who did the secondary research), Hallie Ford, and the late Charles Brand (historical and scenario committee).

Preface

In 1952 Douglas County, Oregon, celebrated its hundredth anniversary. It was my privilege to write the narrative for a four-hour-long pageant, "The Umpqua Cavalcade," to commemorate the spirit of those early pioneers, who brought a wild and untamed country through its infant years, nourished it, and then passed it on. While I found historical facts in state history books, I needed a more personal contact in order to get the feel of the past—a contact with the men and women themselves whose dauntless courage, unity, and faith went largely unsung.

That need took me to the very cradle of the past. I sought out those pioneer people, walked with them, talked with them, and lived with them—however briefly—and in that encounter I saw the beautiful Oregon Country through their eyes and loved it as they loved it. More importantly, I saw its people, whom God had created to have dominion over the paradise it was. "Things were simpler then," they told me; "more gentle."

Can we capture that simplicity? I wondered as I sat on their doorsteps and listened to stories of anguish, tragedy, humor, and irony that they shared. That was the key—*shared!* "We needed each other," they told me, "and we needed to know that God cared."

As the pioneers walked out of my life one by one, having fulfilled their earthly mission with such admirable spirit, the characters in LOVE IS A GENTLE STRANGER walked in—shadowy at first, with no substance. Perhaps I was too caught up with the spirit of all they told me to recognize the characters as mortals with human needs. But as time passed they fleshed out and became so real that they begged to share their story as their real-life forebears had done.

Perhaps you can recapture some of that simplicity in this book. Or perhaps you will find that you have never lost it, in which case the story will serve as a gentle reminder that love is the one force which remains constant. God took care of that through His Son!

As you come to know Chris Beth, who must learn the "New Commandment," Vangie, her "wronged sister," the compelling Wilson North, his patient and compassionate friend, Joseph Craig ("Holy Joe" to Chris Beth!), and the less visible (but nonetheless important) characters, may they bless your life anew. May love in its purest form—though it be a stranger—knock gently and then come into your life

1

Jilted!

The mid-September sun was without mercy. Dust eddied and swirled beneath the horses' hooves, settling on their sweat-lathered bodies as the team strained to pull the stagecoach up the steep mountainside. At times the horses missed their footing on the narrow trail. At those times the coach tilted crazily between the rock face of the mountain and the bottomless canyon below, throwing the six weary-faced passengers rudely against each other. "This heat takes all the energy a body can muster," the capable, prolific looking woman who introduced herself as "Missus Malone" had said some miles back. It was probably to discourage the red-whiskered, gruff-voiced man beside her, Chris Beth supposed. He had been talking since the group had gathered, some four days earlier, to wait for the Northwest bound stage—not that Chris Beth heard anything he or any of the others said. Their words were stifled by the turn of the wheels… *Jilt-ed, jilt-ed,* they jeered.

Jilted. Could there be an uglier word in the dictionary she had brought along? Had sickness or accident claimed Jon, I'd have lived through it, the girl thought. But this—this she could not survive. Not that she cared, as long as there were no knowing friends or relatives around to witness her humility and shame.

"Be ye comin' West to be married?" The Irishman broke the silence. He seemed to be asking the question of her.

Chris Beth shook her head. "To teach," she said, and turned her eyes back to the dusty trail.

"Oh so it's a teacher ye be!" the Irishman exclaimed. "But how be it a pretty thing like you's travelin' alone?"

How be it? Still gazing vacantly at the timber outside the small window somebody had forgotten to curtain properly, Chris Beth tried to put the reason together in her mind…

Jonathan Blake had walked out of her life the way he had walked into it—airily but with determination. Although it had seemed a lifetime, there had been only three months between Jon's passionate whispers against her hair as the lilacs pouted with spring rain. "We have to set the date—I can't wait!" and his equally impassioned plea for release in the magnolia-scented dark of a summer night. How could it be? Jon loved her. He had told her so soon after they met in Boston, his home, where she was finishing teacher training. They were going to be married…invitations were ready…Chris Beth had tried to reach out and touch him, but Jon had moved away. Didn't she hear what he said?

Yes, she had heard. But she didn't believe.

Jon was given to absurd, sudden laughter. That's it—he was teasing! Wasn't he? She had asked.

No. And she was—please—to make it no more painful than it was.

Painful? For which of them? A new and sudden fear had gripped her heart then. *Was there another woman?* Yes.

The wild pounding within her had stopped then. Chris Beth felt her pulse slow to normal—and then stop. Her body might go on living, but her heart had died.

In the white, colorless days that followed, Chris Beth was sure that her body would die too. If I were a praying woman I'd ask for death, she thought as she told her mother there was to be no wedding, and set to work on the grim task of returning the gifts. I'd pray for tears, too; they're supposed to heal. But the hurt was too deep for tears.

Dry-eyed, she carried on. There was no purpose left—just one immediate goal: that of convincing friends that she herself had broken the engagement. After that, she would have to get away. Where, she didn't know—just far, far away.

Her mother was no help, Chris Beth remembered bitterly. She simply paced the long length of the carpeted parlor, wringing her hands and murmuring, "What will people say?" Soothing Mama and rewrapping the presents took a long time. Maybe if Vangie were here to help...but her sister was now in Boston herself, registering for her first year in nursing school. Anyway, Vangie was like Mama—a delightfully pretty lady who swooned at the sight of a mouse. So what was there to do but face this crisis the way she had faced all the others—alone? *Alone.* Then why not be completely alone, away from them all? That's when the idea of coming West came.

Remembering, Chris Beth sucked her hand to choke back hysterical laughter. How ironic that it was Jon himself who gave her the idea! She had listened with a smile to stories he had gathered from wagon masters who were taking immigrants to some place called the Oregon Country. She knew she would never risk her scalp in such untamed wilderness! "Fiddle-dee-dee," she would say when Jon got dangerously carried away with talk of gold, trees big enough to drive a team of horses through, grass belly-deep to the oxen they were driving, and rivers teeming with fish. "Why would civilized, educated people like ourselves choose such a life?" Still, there was a certain gleam in her husband-to-be's eyes that was contagious. Deep inside, Chris Beth recognized an undeveloped sense of adventure in the "self" she believed she inherited from the father who had died before she was born. The one photograph Mama had kept when she remarried showed Chris Beth that father and daughter resembled each other in a dark, straight-browed way. Undoubtedly she was like him in other ways, too—a little withdrawn, and certainly with stronger backbone than her mother.

The thought made Chris Beth square her shoulders. "Why not?" she said aloud. "Yes, why not go West? Pioneer children will have to have teachers." There was no sense of excitement in the decision, no feeling of dedication, no feeling at all. Oregon simply sounded like the farthest place away. Dangers of frontier life no longer mattered. In her numb state, she would welcome death...

Lost in her reverie, Chris Beth had no idea of time. It was a surprise when Mrs. Malone announced, "Suppertime!" Without interest, she watched Mrs. Malone open the giant wicker hamper that had bumped over the dusty trails with them for however many days it had been since the stage had met the train two states back. Food! The idea of eating turned her stomach, but it would be easier to accept a cookie and some fruit than to argue with the well-meaning woman who had tried to mother them all. All I want is a warm bath, a clean bed, and the private world of sleep, she thought. Let the others talk about the beauty of the sunset, the increasing number of fir trees, and the fact that they would cross into Oregon tomorrow. Chris Beth was aware only of a merciful breeze that pushed back her heavy hair and the grind of the wheels that taunted, "Jilted, jilted!"

Covering her ears, Chris Beth dozed fitfully. Her untasted cookie and fruit dropped into crumpled folds of the dark skirt she wore and rolled to the feet of Mrs. Malone.

The older woman shook her head. "I do declare! The child's not eaten a morsel."

In her dreams, Jon returned. The rest of the world slept, and in that hushed and timeless silence the two of them were alone. "My darling!" Jon's arms reached out to embrace her, but she was unable to touch him. Some evil force was pulling him away. "Come back—" Chris Beth tried to call, but Jon was gone, taking the silence with him. Mocking voices beat against her eardrums, indistinct at first, then loud and cruel: "Jilt-ed, Jilt-ed!" Then Jon was back. "My darling!" This time Chris cried out the words of endearment. But Jon was laughing—laughing and mocking her along with the other voices. She tried to run away, but her legs refused to support her. She was falling, only to have a bruising grip imprison her. "No! No!" She must fight against him. But struggling was no good. She was being lifted as if she were a feather, and the arms that held her were gentle—gentle in a way she had never known Jon's arms to be. She tried to look into his eyes, but her weary eyelids drooped. The face was no longer familiar...

2

Forgotten Brooch

Chris Beth awoke as if from a stupor. Someone was shaking her shoulder gently and calling her name, "Christen Elizabeth—Miss Kelly!" Struggling to put the fragments of two worlds together, she tried to remember the voice of the woman who called. Had there been a woman in her dreams? No. And the face she saw as her mind cleared was that of Mrs. Malone. "That's better! Now eat this like a good girl." There was no recourse but to gulp down the warm broth the woman was spooning into her mouth.

"We aren't moving!" Alarmed, Chris Beth tried to sit up. What was she doing lying down in the first place? And where—?

"Whoa, now, take it easy. Broth ain't that potent!"

Chris Beth, who was used to doing things for herself, sank gratefully against the clean, white pillow. She had slept, Mrs. Malone told her, then "just crumpled like." One of the men picked her up from the floor and carried her when they stopped atop the mountain at Half-Way Station.

Half-Way Station? Chris Beth wondered weakly.

It was where the stage changed horses for the rest of the trip.

How long had they been there?

Several hours. "And that's why I woke you. Not enough flesh on them bones to see you through whatever lies ahead."

Chris Beth felt her body grow rigid with fear. The "Injuns and wild b'ar" the men talked about yesterday she could cope with. But having her secret discovered was another matter. "Did I talk—in my sleep, I mean?"

"'Twas a mite more than sleeping—more like delirium. And folks always talk when there's fever. Feel like spongin' off a bit? You missed the tub the keepers fixed last night."

A first emotion stirred within Chris Beth. One had to admire a certain spirit this woman possessed. She did what needed doing and expected nothing in return. Whatever secret she may have revealed was safe with Mrs. Malone. It was still dark outside, but busy sounds from below came through the upstairs window into the bedroom that she and Mrs. Malone must have shared. "Move over, Colonel… this away, Joe…and you, Bill, that away!"

"Hitchin' up. Best you hurry now. The others will want to know the fever's broke. They've been asking."

That the other passengers cared whether she lived or died surprised Chris Beth. What was she to them? She shrugged and poured water from an earthen pitcher into the washbowl. The water's chill surprised her. "Lots of that from here on," Mrs. Malone said. "Fresh off the melted snow." With that, she went to join the others.

Alone in the room, Chris Beth looked at her reflection in the mirror above the washstand and gasped. She was accustomed to kerosene lamps instead of candles. It had to be the difference in light that paled her skin like she had seen the ghost of *Hamlet*. But the light could hardly account for the matted mass of her dark braids or the way her usually ripe-olive eyes had given up their luster.

Maybe a change of clothes—but there was no time. "All aboard!" the driver called. Chris Beth poked hopelessly at her hair and wondered wryly what Indian in his right mind would want it. She snuffed out the candle and hurried down the stairs.

The others were too absorbed by their surroundings to notice she had joined them. All eyes focused on the eastern sky, where rose-tipped fingers of dawn tinted the snowy-capped peaks, pausing where the deep green of the timberline began its gradual slope into the valleys below. One peak in particular seemed to brush the very sky, casting a shadow across what appeared to be a lean-to building. "Lumber camp," someone said, but Chris Beth did not turn around She was watching waterfalls in their cascade from unbelievable heights as if in a hurry to get their journey over and join the river curving around the foot of the mountain range. "That's it! Sure and it is. That be the hill o' home!" The Irishman was near dancing with excitement.

Chris Beth inhaled a lungful of crisp, clean air, a move not to be missed by the red-bearded man. "Ever you see such purity or water so clear?"

She shook her head.

"Flows right by the throne o' God, it does."

Chris Beth moved away. She had no desire to engage herself in an early-morning conversation with the talkative man—let alone about some Supreme Being who had thrown a ball of mud into space and forgotten about the people who inhabited it.

But in spite of herself, Chris Beth felt a strange pull from those majestic mountains. It was as if the whole area and its people were under some kind of magic spell. She shivered. It would be wiser to get aboard than stand there indulging in some silly fantasy.

The driver was bringing a heavy-looking object from Halfway Station. He looked at her for a moment, then asked, "Feel like journeyin' on? Weather's more to our likin'. Still and all, other things can be tryin'."

"I'll be fine," Chris Beth told him.

Still the driver hesitated, pulling at a leather string on his jacket, stroking his month's growth of beard, and spitting intermittently. "That pin," he said finally. "Don't you want I should put it in the strong box?"

Automatically, Chris Beth's hand felt for the brooch where Jon had pinned it—so lovingly, she had thought—the night he proposed. How could she have forgotten to return it when she had remembered all else down to the least detail? And how could she have failed to notice it when she had dressed for the first lap of the journey by train? She had chosen the suit-dress hurriedly, thinking it was the best garment she had for traveling. Most of her wardrobe was for the city.

"Miss?"

"Oh, thank you, yes." Chris Beth tugged at the hateful reminder, forgetting the safety catch, tearing the lace of her stand-up collar, and pricking her finger. "Ouch!" Stronger words of pain rose to her lips—words her all-forbidding stepfather reminded her often enough placed her in danger of "the fires of hell" in his thou-shalt-not form of religion. Not that he had taught her restraint, but something about these simple people told Chris Beth the words were better left unsaid. Anyway, it was consoling to know she could bleed. Maybe hearts weren't all that important, after all.

Handing the pearl and sapphire brooch to the driver, Chris Beth turned toward the open door of the stage. Yes, she would want to guard the expensive piece of jewelry. Nothing must happen to it before they reached the community or town nearest the school where she was to teach. "Then my number one job will be to mail it back to Jonathan Blake!" Chris Beth whispered fiercely.

3

Getting Acquainted

The step into the stagecoach was higher than Chris Beth remembered. She tripped over her long skirt and would have fallen had a familiar masculine hand not steadied her. Familiar? How could it be? But before she could turn to thank the man, others were coming aboard. Try as she would, Chris Beth found herself unable to associate the touch with any of the four men inside, and she and Mrs. Malone were the only women. It was strange, like everything else that was happening to her.

The driver secured the door with one hand, fumbling awkwardly. "Is that a gun?" Chris asked Mrs. Malone, who had rearranged the seating to put Chris Beth beside her.

Mrs. Malone nodded.

"Then there really *are* Indians dodging behind the stumps?"

One of the men laughed. He was younger, she noticed—at least younger than the driver and the other passengers inside. Cleaner, too, she thought, in his red plaid shirt and high boots.

"They're friendly around here for the most part. More curious than anything else about the 'Bostons.'"

"The Bostons?"

"No offense, Miss, if that's where you're from. Out here, we're all 'Bostons' to them—anybody with a pale face."

"Why did the driver take my brooch?" Chris Beth turned to

Mrs. Malone. But it was the young man who answered again. "If we should meet a group of Indians, most likely they will ask for trinkets."

"That was no trinket!"

The young man smiled once more. "Again, no offense, Miss. Their way of putting it."

Chris Beth felt a stir of uneasiness. Mrs. Malone seemed to read her mind. "The gun's not for red men. It's for bandits. This is Black Bart territory."

Chris Beth leaned back and inhaled deeply, trying to take it all in. So this was Oregon Country. Although her unfeeling heart refused to appreciate her surroundings, even then she realized that it was a land of strange contrasts—one that was bound to bring out the best or the worst in its inhabitants.

"I expect you'll be wanting to know more about the settlement where we're going." Mrs. Malone's words were a statement more than a question.

"I suppose I'll need to know."

The older woman removed her yarn and knitting needles from a paisley bag, counted to herself until the needles seemed to move under their own power, and began a monologue. "We're few in number, but close-knit like. Neighbors all pitch in and do what's to get itself done in good times and bad. Lots of women can't adjust—just kind of pale up and die like, or else go back to wherever home is. Me, I never give it much thought. Home's here, but then I been here most of my life. Ma and Pa's buried in the little plot down by Graveyard Creek right near the school. That's where you'll be teachin'."

It occurred suddenly to Chris Beth that this woman knew a lot about her—her name and where she would teach (if she got the contract, and she dared not think of what would happen if she didn't). But why was Mrs. Malone speaking of "we"? Was it possible she would be a neighbor? Oh, she hoped so! She hoped so very much. There would be need of such a warm, friendly person in this strange, new life.

Mrs. Malone must have read her thoughts. "You'll be wonderin' how I got my facts. I'm not given to meddlin'."

"Oh, I never thought that!" Chris Beth protested.

"Well, you had just cause. But when you taken sick like, somebody had to take over and me being the only other woman—"

Chris Beth felt a flow of shame. She had forgotten to thank Mrs. Malone.

"I appreciated that." Chris Beth reached to touch the busy, work-reddened hands whose rhythm never stopped.

"Not necessary in the settlement. Neighborliness is our way of survivin'. But there's need to explain the intrusion. I asked of the driver concernin' you. And anyway I'd guessed a'ready. News travels amongst us, you know. We'd heard about the southern-born schoolma'm, even your name, so when I saw the initials on your handbag—" Mrs. Malone paused to pull out a new ball of red yarn.

"Do you live near the school somewhere?" Chris Beth asked hopefully.

"Close as neighbors get, just several homesteads away. A married man was entitled to a square mile of land when Pa staked his claim. Bachelors could hold half as much, and most of 'em never got developed without a missus, so there's a heap of timber between."

The Irishman who had been patting his foot to some remembered tune suddenly burst out:

Me hates all women, and yet it be plain,

Me must marry soon, or lose half me claim!

Mrs. Malone silenced him with a look. "Men outnumber women folks nine to one," she said meaningfully, " 'specially since the gold rush. Even so, we manage. Boys've learned to do a man's work, and that's good in my circumstances. Ned and Jed took over when my husband took to his death. And now with Jed gone—"

Her voice broke slightly. "But you've troubles enough. Why'm I bothering you with mine?"

"Until now, it's been the other way around—and it's no bother,"

Chris Beth said, meaning it. It was a relief to get her mind off herself, even temporarily. "When will Jed be coming home?"—

"He's home a'ready." Mrs. Malone's voice was barely audible over the bump of the wheels. "Mine caved in. I been away—burying him."

The simplicity of the statement caught Chris Beth off guard. It would be easier to cry for this acceptant, stouthearted woman than for herself if her dry eyes could produce tears.

"I'm so sorry," she said softly. "I didn't know."

"Course you didn't." Mrs. Malone drew out a handkerchief with a tattered edge, blew her nose, then folded it away. "Life's like that—rain and sun all mingled, with a whole passel of rainbows in between. Sometimes I think it's the smiles and tears all stirred up together that makes 'em so brilliant."

I want to remember that, Chris Beth thought. It would be something worth sharing with the students if it rained as much in Oregon as people said.

That thought led to another. Clearing her throat, Chris Beth confided as steadily as she could that there was no guarantee she would be teaching—no contract, anyway, but just a letter from a trustee saying, in response to her inquiry, that there was need for a teacher. She might have added that she was barely able to read even that much of a pencil-scribbled message on the back of a supply list which Mr. Goldsmith had sent.

"Well don't go borrowin' trouble. Nate Goldsmith's as good as his name. And once he sees you, there can't be any questioning. He'll make a grab for you."

"Right!"

Chris Beth felt herself blush under the younger man's single word of appreciation, but she supposed she should not be offended.

"My, my!" Mrs. Malone looked from one of the young people to the other. "We've been under the same roof a spell now and it appears to me we ought to introduce ourselves proper like. Never occurred to me we'd all be headin' so far together."

"Wilson, you do the honor while I unpack us some lunch."

He glanced at Mrs. Malone. "Yessum!" he said in mock obedience, then spoke to the others. "As you see, the two of us know each other. I'm Wilson North and the young lady—"

"Seems they all know Miss Kelly," Mrs. Malone broke in. "Tell them about your book, Wilson, and that you're studyin' to be a—"

A lurch of the stage tilted the hamper dangerously in Mrs. Malone's lap, interrupting her sentence.

"I'm a botanist, studying plant life."

Chris Beth acknowledged with a nod, wondering how he and Mrs. Malone knew each other.

Wilson North turned to the Irishman. "O'Higgin?"

"Sure and that be my name, Irish and Scotch, but a man of mild habits."

"'Tis true," Mrs. Malone agreed as she laid out the fried chicken, fresh bread, pickles, and coconut layer cake from the basket she had replenished at Half-Way Station.

Chris Beth missed the mumbled names of the other men, gathering only that they were fur trappers She was puzzling over Mrs. Malone's obvious acquaintance with the man who called himself simply O'Higgin. Maybe there were even fewer settlers in the Northwest than she had supposed.

Mrs. Malone packed away the remnants of lunch. Wilson North and O'Higgin talked about the tall stand of Douglas fir mingled with giants of the forest (redwood trees, she overheard them say), and they identified mountain ash (now bright with crimson berries), manzanita, and laurel. Occasionally Chris Beth looked to where the two men pointed and wondered how the noonday sun was able to penetrate the foliage enough to cast a shadow. The same sense of awe and mystery she had sensed at Half-Way Station returned—something she was unable to identify. Tired as she was, in an irrational sort of way she wished they could stay in the cramped quarters of the stagecoach and just ride.

Mrs. Malone interrupted any question she might have asked.

"Now then," she said as she resumed her knitting, "we'd best be thinkin' of where you'll stay. Would you like to come home with me till you settle in?"

Settle in? But where? Chris Beth realized that she had taken care of the little things but had neglected the ones that mattered.

"I—I thought—surely there's a place to board?"

Her words must have sounded ridiculous, for the others looked at her in surprise. Mrs. Malone simply shook her head. "Nothin'. And the nearest town—store, really—is a day's wagon ride."

All the bravado that Chris Beth had felt back in the city was gone. Here she was in the wilderness alone and frightened out of her wits. She had nobody to lean on, even if she had been a leaner! But going back was out of the question.

"'Twill all turn out according to the Lord's will. You got no cause to worry. Just be glad you know Him!"

This woman spoke as if she and her God were personally acquainted. Well, she found no comfort in such thinking. Maybe she should correct whatever wrong impression she had given, but she felt last night's weakness seeping into her bones, squeezing her heart, and dragging her dry eyelids closed. Wearily, she leaned back and waited for the wheels of the stagecoach to resume their hateful rhythm.

But the disturbing words did not come. Instead, she dreamed a beautiful dream. In it, a man she had never met was reaching out to her. She took his hand. The touch was gentle and they were strangers no longer...

4

End of the World

Chris Beth awoke. The stagecoach had stopped in the middle of the green maze she had seen from a distance at Half-Way Station. She shuddered as she remembered the myths and half-truths she had heard about Black Bart's gang of "polite robbers." But the freckled boy (about 11, she judged) looked innocent enough. He stood awkwardly beside the wagon and waved.

Passengers began picking up their belongings. Everybody talked at once. Chris Beth was hurdled through the open door, where the driver waited. He reached a gloved hand to help her from the stage.

"Trail ends here," he told her. Then, turning to a man climbing down from the driver's seat, he said, "Good havin' you, Joe. Better turn back to Redding with me."

"Another time, Hank."

Mrs. Malone, who had moved up beside Chris Beth, followed her gaze. "That's Joseph Craig. Remember?" No, she didn't remember him nor would she remember him the next time. All she saw was a faded trademark where overall suspenders crossed his back. Chris Beth was aware only of the man's immense height.

"He rode atop—'Shotgun Messenger,' you know, protectin' the treasure box and mail." A responsible position, Chris supposed, but her concern was for herself and where she was going.

"This away, Miss Mollie!" The boy called from the wagon. Mrs. Malone waved to him.

"That's Ned. Come on, folks! Room for us all."

O'Higgin picked up one of the bags the driver had taken from under the canvas cover in back of the stage and had placed at Mrs. Malone's feet. "This be yours?" At the woman's nod, the Irishman headed for the wagon.

Chris Beth felt a sense of embarrassment when she saw Wilson North pick up her two bags and hand one to Ned Malone—no, not Malone. The boy had said "Miss Mollie"…."Anything more, Miss?" Wilson North asked. Chris Beth felt her face flush.

"No!" she answered with an edge to her voice. So they all thought her helpless because she was new to this part of the world—some Southern belle or china doll unable to do anything for herself. Well, she'd show them.

But the resolve was short-lived. "M-Miss Kelly, I—I believe this is yours?" Chris Beth did not recognize the slight stammer, but she turned and found herself looking into the eyes of the "man from up top." Joseph Craig pointed toward the driver's seat as if to introduce himself, then reddened when he seemed to realize he had gestured with the object he was handing her. *The brooch! How could I have forgotten—again?* But before she could thank the shy young man, he had placed the pin in her hand and picked up her satchel. Chris Beth realized furiously that Wilson North was watching with a little smile of amusement. She dropped the pin in her bag and snapped it shut.

"Miss Kelly will ride with you, Ned," Mrs. Malone said. "Mind your manners, son, and help her now. I'll ride—no, come to think on it, Miss Kelly had best ride in the spring seat behind us. There's a heap of talkin' you and I need to do."

Chris Beth noted with relief that Wilson North had positioned himself beside O'Higgin at the back of the wagon bed. Apparently, the two men would ride backward, dangling their feet. The trappers had disappeared into the woods. That left Joseph Craig, and, although she didn't know him, Chris Beth felt that anybody was to be preferred to the man who seemed to delight in her helplessness. How much did he know of her past?

But there was no time to dwell on the past or even on the future. Chris Beth was too busy viewing the strange new world around her. As the team left the main road, they entered an even denser forest, the wagon wheels moving soundlessly over the dry needles that covered the narrow road. Once her eyes adjusted to the underwater green of the light, the country was even more beautiful than the wagon masters had described it. Fir trees brushed the sky in their reach for light, and head-high ferns huddled around their trunks, providing refuge for squirrels that flitted everywhere. Rabbits, unafraid, went on with their play, and once a skunk strolled dangerously near. Nobody seemed to notice, not even when the antlered deer stood watching curiously as the wagon passed.

Chris Beth watched in fascination as the timber crowded in, then widened out a bit to let the wagon through. How lovely!

The man beside her had the good sense not to talk. While she was grateful for her seatmate's silence, it seemed unnatural somehow. Now and then Chris Beth stole a look at him. His expression told her nothing. It was an interesting face, she decided—even handsome, she supposed, in a craggy sort of way. Once, sensing her gaze, Joseph Craig turned. Then he glanced away shyly. But for a brief moment their gazes held. *He reminds me of somebody,* she thought. But try as she would, she could remember no man with such kind, blue eyes. Something in that brief glance told Chris Beth this man would understand her need to share appreciation for this mysterious, ruggedly beautiful land—without talking it to death.

"It's so unspoiled, so unused," she ventured.

Joseph Craig did not disappoint her. "Exactly," he said, and fell silent again.

The fir boughs sighed above them, and somewhere below water rippled in a sort of lullaby. *Restful.* That would have been more like it. The feeling that Chris Beth had in the stagecoach returned. She wished that if life had to go on, it could continue like this. Her tired eyes rested on the eternal green canopy. Her ears listened gratefully to its whisper. Yes, it would be nice, just going on forever. But somewhere beyond all this was a real world to deal with. Already light appeared ahead.

"Will we reach the settlement soon?"

"An hour at most," Joseph Craig promised. "We—we've been traveling about two hours."

Two hours! With another to go? *Three hours from civilization—if one could call the stagecoach civilization!* The forest had soothed her, maybe soothed her dangerously. It would be easy to be mesmerized in this mysterious country where hours flew.

"Look!" Joseph Craig pointed below to where the canyon dipped dangerously. Near-toppled trees, twining their roots in the rocks along the steep walls, somehow managed to hold on. At the bottom of the canyon, a raging river twisted and writhed, as if trying to straighten out its powerful body in its tortuous journey to the sea. *Such force!* Chris Beth shivered.

"Awesome, but one of our lifelines," he volunteered in the quiet voice she had come to appreciate: "Trout, even salmon on their way to spawn early in the year. Lots of our water comes from here too—sometimes too much as you can see," he nodded at the bare roots hanging above the river. "Water table's close to the surface, so most have wells. My place has a spring. Oh! there it is—" and there was excitement in Joseph's voice

Following his gaze, Chris Beth gasped with pleasure. Far below, the road dipped sharply into a sudden, sunlit clearing. The grass-carpeted valley, hugged by mountains—purple in the distance—divided, like a nine-patch quilt with threads of blue water. The "patches" must be individual homesteads, she supposed. The whole scene looked more like a painting on Mama's wall than a settlement. One proud frame house stood apart, and here and there she was able to pick out a log cabin. Flowers filled the yards. Vines—grapes, she was to learn later—curved along the eaves. The only signs of life were tendrils of smoke rising from fat, rock chimneys of the little houses.

"Most likely smoking jerky," Joseph said to her unasked question.

Jerky? There is so much I'll need to learn—but she had missed something Joseph Craig said.

"—alone since then. See the one that's mine?"

A small cabin stood where he pointed. But as to why he was alone she had missed.

"Oh, it's beautiful—beautiful," Chris Beth said of the valley and wished desperately for Jon—or the person she had thought him to be—to share it with her. But she would never be able to share anything again—not really—especially her heart.

Chris Beth felt the eyes of Joseph Craig fixed on her. It was unsettling. Had she spoken aloud? Surely not—but why was he staring? From the corner of her eye Chris Beth saw concern in the man's face. Well, she didn't want his pity—.

"Whoa!" Ned tightened his hold on the reins, and the wagon stopped.

They were in front of the big frame house, and suddenly it looked lonely. To Chris Beth's dismay, the cabins, which had appeared huddled together, were swallowed up by the forest. *End of the trail,* the driver had called it. More like the end of the world! She shivered again, then squared her shoulders in what she hoped covered all misgivings. She stood up quickly and jumped lightly to the ground before any of the men could help her.

"M-Miss Kelly," Joseph spoke with a little uncertainty; "you left your handbag."

The words, though soft, were not lost to Wilson North. Stopping in midstretch after the long ride in back of the wagon bed, he acknowledged her presence with a little nod, his half-smile mocking and his eyes, though twinkling, mentally calculating her telltale signs of inadequacy.

Chris Beth grabbed the bag angrily and stalked away. *The man was impossible!*

5

An Empty Chair

An unmistakable aroma of coffee filled the air, plus something else that Chris Beth was unable to identify. The yeasty smell reminded her of Mama's "light bread," or was it the delivery wagon from which she used to purchase raised rolls? For the first time in weeks, she felt hungry.

"The welcoming committee!" Mrs. Malone warned. Suddenly the travelers were surrounded by several children and a wolflike dog. The children tripped over one another in their rush to reach Mrs. Malone first, and the dog alternated between barking and checking out the newcomers and scents on the wagon wheels.

After she had embraced each child in turn, Mrs. Malone blew her nose, wiped her eyes, and became her efficient self again. "Now, Lola Ann, step up front," she said to the tallest of the girls, "and bring Jimmy John." Suddenly aware of an audience, the children stopped their chatter. Awkwardly, Lola Ann came forward, leading a dumpling shaped boy who tried to hide behind her calico skirt.

"Lola Ann's the oldest and Jimmy John's the baby. This is Amelia, and—Harmony, where are you hidin'? She's our shyest. After her, there's Andrew—he's helpin' unhitch the team. And then, there are—was—the twins. Now there's Ned."

The children greeted the men but their eyes, fastened on Chris Beth, were round with fright. "Scamper now." At Mrs. Malone's command they hurried gratefully away. "Set up places for Wilson and Joe. One for Miss Kelly, too," she called behind them. Turning to her guests, she invited, "Come into the front room. And, Wolf, stop that silly barkin'!" But Chris Beth saw Mrs. Malone pat the dog on the head affectionately.

Chris Beth wondered as they filed into the big room how Mrs. Malone kept all the names straight. *And how,* she thought, *does she manage to handle grief so matter-of-factly?* It was as if the routine of a meal were of more consequence than a death in the family. *We're cut off a different bolt,* she thought, then desperately, *I'll never be able to make it here!*

There was no time to look around the "front room," as Mrs. Malone called the parlor, except to note that curtains were drawn against the noon sun. Lola Ann appeared at the door, wiping her damp hands on her apron, to announce that dinner was ready.

"Miss Kelly—" Mrs. Malone began.

"Chris Beth, please, Mrs. Malone."

"Chris Beth," her hostess said without hesitation, "you can wash in the basin. You men wash at the outside pump."

That's the way things are out here, Chris Beth thought, splashing her face gratefully with water. *A friendship offered is a friendship accepted without reservation.* She remembered that in her upbringing strangers were outsiders until established families checked "background and breeding." Well, Western ways were to her advantage. No fear here of people's finding out what she chose to keep to herself. But even with her mixed-up emotions, which kept volleying back and forth, Chris Beth felt a certain sense of warmth that she had missed in her childhood.

Wilson North pulled a chair from the long table, and Chris Beth found herself seated without so much as a "by your leave" right beside him. Mrs. Malone took her place at the foot of the table and motioned for Joseph Craig to sit at her right side. O'Higgin appeared to seat himself at her left. Strange that Mrs. Malone had made no mention of his being a guest. He must be a frequent visitor.

"Amelia, have all you children had your meal?" The girl nodded. " 'cept Ned—"

Ned was hesitating at the dining room door. Was he uncomfortable before company or was there something else? Chris Beth watched the boy move toward the head of the table and pause.

Mrs. Malone shook her head. "You're the oldest boy now, 'tis true. Still and all, you're not the one to take your papa's place."

The boy looked relieved, Chris Beth thought, as he left the empty chair. He sat down and bowed his head. She looked around the table and saw that all the others had bowed their heads, too. Quickly, she lowered her eyes.

"O'Higgin?" The way Mrs. Malone spoke was a request.

"Lord, we be thankin' Ye for this food," the Irishman responded. "And we be askin' Ye to bless all the people within the walls of this hoose."

"House!" Mrs. Malone corrected. "Amen."

Chris Beth glanced up to see if there was a smile anywhere. Catching her eye, Wilson North lifted an eyebrow in shared amusement. Well, I'll not respond to that, she thought hotly, and busied herself trying to scoop a helping of mashed potatoes from the mountain set before her without tearing it down and giving him cause for a belly laugh!

As the girls brought bowl after bowl of garden-fresh vegetables, venison, and hot coffee, her appetite increased. Then came the enormous plate of biscuits! She knew immediately that they were the source of the yeasty aroma that had welcomed her arrival. "If I take one, I'll split at the seams," she smiled at Amelia. "But if I don't, I'll die of curiosity."

"So might as well enjoy your demise," Wilson North said, laying one of the fluffy, golden-crowned biscuits on her plate. "I'll give you a starter."

"Starter of what?"

"Sourdough. You'll need it for biscuits like these. It's what the prospectors use in place of milk. You *can* cook?"

Chris Beth buttered her biscuit. Whether she could cook was none of this man's business!

To hide her irritation, Chris Beth turned her eyes to the head of the table and the hauntingly empty chair. The emptiness seemed to symbolize something to her, but she was unable to attach to it anything she remembered. She wondered about it. She wondered, too, which of the children belonged to Mrs. Malone and about a lot of other things. Why had the older woman forgotten to tell the children she might be their teacher? Or maybe they knew. Everybody else seemed to. Then, for the first time, she wondered how O'Higgin, Wilson North, and Joseph—she had come to think of him as Joe—happened to be on the same stagecoach that brought the neighboring Mrs. Malone to the settlement.

The girls began to clear the table, and Chris Beth saw that the two younger men were preparing to leave. "How far away are they from you?" she asked Mrs. Malone as they picked up their gear.

"Four miles across the creek," she replied. "The horses will meet them somewhere in the woods, I expect, and sort of save their legs."

The two men must live close together, thought Chris Beth. Joe swung his pack easily over his shoulder. "Miss Kelly, if you wish, I—I'll take you to see Nate tomorrow."

"Oh, would you?" Chris Beth answered quickly. She could plan nothing at all until she met the trustee and found out for sure if she had a teaching job.

"Of course," he said. "It will do the buggy good to get s-some exercise." She noticed that Joe had returned to his slight stammer. Back in the forest, it had disappeared.

Wilson broke into her thoughts. "Shucks! I was planning you and *I* would go calling on Nate. Or don't you like horseback riding—double, that is?"

At that moment, Chris Beth found nothing about this man particularly to her liking and she hoped her cold glance said as much! Mrs. Malone saved the moment. "The Lord will bless you both—you, too, O'Higgin—for what you did for me," she said.

Joe placed his arm around her shoulders. "It was nothing at all," he said.

Then, as Wilson brushed the woman's cheek lightly with his lips, Chris Beth noticed a change of expression. She could have sworn there were tears in his eyes.

She shook her head in wonderment, suddenly very tired. It had been a strange day.

6

Secret Desires

Early-morning sun was tinting the front-room windows (where Mrs. Malone had made down a temporary bed for Chris Beth) when Joe came for her. Fortunately, she had awakened early, brushed and braided her hair, and put on a fresh white blouse. The rumpled suit would have to do until she found a place to unpack and sort her other clothing. The blouse needed an ornament at the neck, but there was no time to rummage through her grip, and certainly she wouldn't be wearing the brooch! Thought of the brooch was a reminder that she would have to check on the mail service. The sooner it was on its way to Jon, the better. Let the "other woman" have it, she thought bitterly.

As Chris Beth wound her braids into a crown and secured them with combs, she had time to look about the great room which had served as a bedroom. The ceilings were high and beamed with mellow rafters. The fireplace looked large enough for the entire family to gather around, and Chris Beth wondered what purpose the big black pot suspended in its mouth served. On the east side of the room, just beyond the dining room door, a wide staircase with polished banisters led upstairs. The upstairs rooms were unfinished, Mrs. Malone had said last night, "with beds wedged in amongst the packin' crates."

Did they plan to finish the room? Chris Beth wondered. "Yes—in time—busy workin' out details when the children's papa died."

Chris Beth realized later that the older woman must have sensed her questions. She was such a perceptive person. Mr. Malone had been a widower when Mollie met him, she explained of her late husband. A man with six children "a'growin" needed a mate, and she, a spinster, needed somebody to love after "layin' away" both parents. And, besides, there was Turn-Around Inn to take care of.

Turn-Around Inn?

Mrs. Malone's eyes misted with tears as she recalled, "This very house. It was his dream, and maybe it'll come true yet, if the railroad comes on through. Only the good Lord knows. Time was when folks talked of bringin' steamboats up the river. Passengers could've linked up with the stage. But," she sighed, "roads and rails stopped 'bout the same time."

Mrs. Malone had straightened her shoulders then. "Good years, but past." Chris Beth marveled again at the woman's ability to put life in its proper perspective. "Meantime, I've got me a mighty wholesome family! And Turn-Around Inn's name turned out to be just the right name for Papa's house." Mrs. Malone bit her lip in concentration. "Wasn't for that I could put you up proper-like right here. But," she continued determinedly, "the Lord's work comes first."

"I guess I don't understand," Chris Beth said slowly.

"'Course you don't. 'Twould take another Solomon to unriddle some of my sayin's sometimes. You see, folks here in the settlement have no place to worship when the rains come. Till then we use a brush arbor down by Graveyard Creek. Later it floods like the river. So we use the front room here."

Mrs. Malone had told more about her neighbors, but Chris Beth's weary mind absorbed little of it—at least, little that she could recall this morning. Wilson North and Joseph Craig were close friends, both "bound over by profession"—wasn't that the phrase she had used? Both had "suffered deeply" with pox epidemic, and O'Higgin was like "kinfolks" to the Malones. Chris Beth had dozed off while her hostess was explaining how he and the two younger men refused to let her face Jed's burial alone, "even with them tryin' to finish school and all."

All this Chris Beth was mulling over as she readied herself for the trip to see Nate Goldsmith. The rich smell of brewing coffee told her that Mrs. Malone's keen ears had heard her movements and that she was downstairs starting breakfast. Hurriedly, Chris Beth tried to roll up the feather bed the way it had been the night before. She was still struggling with it when she heard Mrs. Malone answer Joe's knock at the front hall door.

"Couldn't have slept much," she heard Mrs. Malone confide. "But she's an independent one—refusin' to take one of the girls' beds."

"Here, let me help." Joe appeared at the front-room door. He looked different wearing a white shirt and tie, and again Chris Beth was aware of his enormous height. She noticed, too, the strength of his hands as with an effortless flip he dispensed with the feather bed. Yet he didn't make her feel helpless.

After the biggest breakfast of her life—who could resist feather-light sourdough pancakes, all crispy-brown around the edges, surrounded by homemade sausages?—and a final cup of coffee, the two of them climbed into the buggy. At Joe's "Go, Dobbin Girl!" the gray mare trotted toward the wooded area that Chris Beth had seen the two men enter the evening before.

Suddenly it was as if they were beneath a multicolored umbrella. Autumn had come early to the area, surprising Chris Beth with its brilliance. Every tree seemed to lean toward the buggy, linking limbs as if to form a gold-and-crimson canopy above the passengers. The beauty of it all made Chris Beth's heart ache. She remembered the rides that she and Jon had taken together on Sunday afternoons, with the horse cantering along the avenue while, heads together, they had talked of their lives together…

Well, she wasn't going to think of him—not about him or the uncertainties that lay ahead. Today was enough. On impulse, she touched Joe's sleeve. "Oh, can't we stop a minute—I mean, can we? I just want to walk in the leaves!"

"Whoa Dobbin!" The gray mare stopped on the trail. "I can understand." And Joe smiled.

Together they walked without talking beneath the bright arch, dry leaves crunching and disintegrating under their shoes. They gathered armloads of brilliant branches and filled the box on the buggy. Maybe it *was* good she had come here. Maybe—

"Oh, we must go," Chris Beth interrupted her own thinking with genuine regret.

Joe nodded. "I'm glad we stopped, though." He paused, and she knew he wanted to say more. *Oh, now don't spoil it,* her heart begged. She needn't have worried. What Joe Craig said was, "I wouldn't want you hugging a secret desire like mine. Take a look at the staircase back at Mrs. Malone's."

"It's lovely."

"Every single time I go there I have a feeling I'd like to slide down the banister!"

Chris Beth heard the echo of their laughter even after they had climbed back into the buggy and continued toward the Goldsmith place. Strange, she was to think later, that there would have been no feeling of premonition of what was to destroy her beginning sense of belonging.

7

Bound By Contract— And Mountains

A covered bridge spanned Graveyard Creek. Nate Goldsmith heard Dobbin clopping over the loose boards and came to the edge of the clearing to meet Chris Beth and Joe. Chris Beth could see that the man was expecting them. His sparse hair looked like he had dipped his head in the rain barrel, but he had overlooked a thin brown coffee trail that parted his beard like a fork. His one suspender looked ready to pop its button as he leaned against the rail fence.

"Shut up, Coon Dog!" he ordered a barking hound. The animal slunk toward the small cabin, causing the chickens to squawk and take to the air. "You, too!" he called after them. Then, turning to his guests, the school trustee motioned them inside.

"Company fer dinner, Ole Lady!" he called before introducing himself to Chris Beth. But, for all his bluster, she sensed in this man the same kindness she had appreciated among her other new acquaintances. Their acceptance humbled her.

Nate shook hands with Joe, addressing him as "Brother Joseph," and told Chris Beth she was "mighty purty." "I'd ask that we sit a spell, 'cept dinner's most ready and I don't take a shine to talkin' bizness on a empty stomach."

Nate Goldsmith's wife, a small, birdlike woman, made a quick appearance and acknowledged the introduction briefly, her words sounding like a mixture of German and French, and then darted away. She returned only to serve the simple meal.

"Ask the blessin', Brother Joseph, and let's eat," Nate said.

To Chris Beth's surprise, Joe bowed his head. "Lord, we thank You for this day and all its blessings in this land of plenty. We especially thank You for bringing the teacher we needed so much. Give her strength for the job ahead. In the name of Your Son. Amen."

Chris Beth was touched by the simple prayer, even though it disturbed her to be mentioned by name. It was as if Joe were asking his Lord to test her, instead of leaving the matter to the board of trustees! She had noticed, too, that there was no hesitancy in Joe's speech as he prayed. Maybe it was because he was at ease instead of having to weigh words. Well, why should it matter that he and God were on good terms? It shouldn't—but it did.

Nate Goldsmith finished an apple dumpling and pushed his chair back from the table. Looking sharply at Chris Beth, he asked, "Do you reckon as how you can lick 'em an' larn 'em?"

Startled, she nodded. Somewhere in the background there were stifled giggles. So there were children? Better trained than the hound and the chickens, apparently!

Chris Beth realized that the self-appointed "President of the Board" was talking—and that he had little but bad news. As a teacher, she would be entitled to 50 dollars a month "less'n crops fail and folks can't meet taxes." The school term would last about six months, "dependin' on crops," but he wondered aloud if she could last the year out. There had been those, he observed darkly, who hadn't. All this was providing Chris Beth could pass the teachers' exam.

"We're a state now," he said with pride, then paused for an answer to something. The exam?

Yes, she thought she could pass.

And was she willing to abide by other stipulations?

Well, yes—

"They bein'," Nate told her, "that you conduct yourself at all times like a lady, partake in church and general bizness of the settlement, pull yer share of the work on the grounds and general upkeep—oh, somethin' else, contract's null and void iffen you marry."

Chris Beth felt Joe's eyes on her and blushed. "I have no intention of marrying," she said stiffly. *Now or ever!*

"Well, then, I'm right pleased to welcome you amongst us. No need fer signin' a paper. Figger yer word's good as mine. Anyway, havin' witnesses like we did," Nate looked at Joe, then jerked his head toward the kitchen, where his "Ole Lady" was washing dishes quietly, "binds us legal enough."

Did she have any questions?

Well, there was a matter of a place to stay.

Cabin on the school grounds. Needed some fixing up, but— "Could we stop by?" Chris Beth asked Joe.

He looked at the lowering sun. "Better make it another time," he said.

"Oh, the exam," Chris Beth remembered as they prepared to leave.

"Ill tend to that come next Tuesday. The ole lady will be needin' some supplies and I kin pick up a copy at Jed's General Store. You folks need somethin'?"

The trip was a day's wagon ride from the settlement, Chris Beth remembered Mrs. Malone had said. The brooch simply *had* to be on its way to Jon.

"Would it be possible for you to mail a package for me?"

Nate weighed the question, then shook his head doubtfully. "Be glad to 'commodate, Miss Kelly. But there's no tellin' when 'twould go. Like as not mail's delivered by horseback over the hump. Reminds me, though, I'd best be checkin' to see what mail's come fer the settlement since last month."

Month! Had she heard right? Slowly, amazement gave way to disappointment, and then despair. Returning the brooch was the most important thing in her life!

Gone was the mellow mood of the day. The mysterious hills were no longer friendly. They were sentinels, holding her captive.

Chris Beth felt a peculiar sensation of lost hope. But hope of *what?* Escape? No, the stagecoach, irregular and slow as it was, offered a means of departure. It had to be something else. Then, with a flood of shame, she realized the awful truth. Sending Jon's gift back would have done more than finish up the love affair. The package would have given him her whereabouts—offered an opportunity for him to get in touch, beg her forgiveness, and ask for a chance for them to begin a new life in the land he had dreamed of.

"Can I do anything for you, Miss Kelly?" Joe's blue eyes were full of compassion as they waved goodbye to Nate.

Yes, ask your God to hurry along with that strength you asked Him for! she thought wildly. Aloud she said, "I'm fine. Really, I am."

But her smile was too bright—like the autumn leaves which even now were twisting on their fragile stems and dropping one by one to wither and die.

"Oh, Joe—" A little sob caught in her throat.

He placed a gentle hand on her shoulder. Automatically, she touched it with her own hand.

8

A Strange Tranquility

The week that followed was busy, and for that Chris Beth was grateful. She had settled, she found, into the unfeeling pattern established when she went through the motions of canceling wedding plans. She was here, bound by contract, and there was no money to go back home even if she could face the situation she had run away from.

As for returning the brooch—yes, of course the painful reminder of false love had to go. It would be too late, but in her heart she knew its return would be of no consequence anyway. How she could get it back to Jon was another matter, but it was too valuable to leave lying in some store whose owner she had never met with no idea as to when it would be mailed.

Maybe someday, I'll feel it's better this way, she told herself. But for now she had no feeling at all, except for the familiar cold emptiness. *I should never have allowed a notion that life would be better here.* She bit her lip but was aware of no pain—just the salty taste of blood.

"Somethin' troubling you?" Chris Beth had failed to hear Mrs. Malone come into the front room, where she was sorting through her clothes.

Certain that her confusion showed, Chris Beth mumbled that her dresses were in bad shape and wondered vaguely if what she had brought would be suitable.

"Well *that's* no cause for worry. I'm finished churnin' and have the irons heatin' on the stove. I'll help," she said, picking up a blue woolen dress and smoothing it with her hands.

I must show more feeling, even if I have to fake it. "Thank you, Mrs. Malone," she said warmly. "Is this lace collar too dressy for school?"

"I've a piece of natural linen in the chest. Think I'll whip up collar and cuffs. It'll take less than a jiffy."

"I'm grateful. Sewing is not among my skills. I *can* cook, though," she added, wondering why she felt it necessary to defend herself. "'I pestered Cook until she let me help in the kitchen. Mostly, a seamstress made our clothes at first. And all the fancywork was done by Mama and Vangie. You should have seen my *trousseau*—"Chris Beth sucked in her breath, aghast at what she had said.

Mrs. Malone bit off a thread and mercifully backed the conversation up. "Vangie?"

Chris Beth exhaled gratefully. "My younger sister—half sister—Evangeline. Mama remarried after my father was killed."

Mrs. Malone, squinting to thread her needle, nodded. "Probably wise."

"Not really!" Chris Beth felt the familiar bitterness beg for release. "Mama hadn't recovered from her loss. My father was an engineer—gone a lot, and finally killed in an explosion. She married on the rebound. He—*Father* Stein, the name to his liking—represented safety." Chris Beth felt her pulse quicken hatefully. No wonder Mama complained of palpitations.

Mrs. Malone leaned forward. "Was it so awful you can't forgive?" she asked softly.

"Forgive!" Something exploded inside Chris Beth's chest, and release came. "It was obedience he wanted. He was a bigot and a hypocrite." She stopped briefly, forcing herself to lower her voice: "Conscientious and devout, but *cruel!*"

Memories, too long suppressed, flooded back with tidalwave force—the self-righteous pseudorector who considered all others his parish to bend to his will, shaking a warning finger at Chris Beth and Vangie, his voice raised in final judgment at the slightest childish provocation. "Everlasting torment is just a breath away. Now pray, both of you, *pray!*" Vangie's fragile face would pale. Her thin, little figure would crouch pitifully at her father's feet—like a tiny, fallen angel. And always her almost-inaudible words sought forgiveness of that condemning man—not his God. On those frequent occasions, Chris Beth refused to yield. It came as natural as breathing to try to protect the younger girl in the only way she knew. "Let her alone!" she would sob, beating at his bulky middle with her small fists. Mama, who was "delicate since the children's birth," would come down with one of her headaches. Vangie was dragged away, and Chris Beth—an "instrument of the devil"—was locked in the attic to "meditate on the Scriptures." She shuddered as she remembered the old Bible prophecies that Father Stein (whom she refused to call by that doubtful title) chose for her to read. And, oh, the awful nightmares that followed...

A merry whistle announced that O'Higgin, his woodcutting done for the day, was "home" for supper. "Sakes alive! How time does fly when we women get sewin' and talkin'!" Mrs. Malone brought Chris Beth back to the warm present and the tantalizing smell of rising sourdough biscuits.

Gratefully she looked around the friendly room, where her ready-for-school dresses lined the walls. She had half-expected to see the menacing face of her mother's husband looming above. Her lip tasted salty again and her hands were clenched into white-knuckled fists, but something rarefying and sweet had happened inside—something clean, pure, and good. The terrible nightmare was over.

"Oh, Mrs. Malone! How can I thank you?"

"No need. The past is an all-right place to visit on occasion, but we don't want it to nest in our hair." Mrs. Malone patted her shoulder and moved capably toward the dining room, where Lucy Ann was coaxing the last of summer's zinnias into a vase. "Real pretty—"

then, raising her voice, "O'Higgin, take off your shoes and don't go trackin' the scrubbed floor!"

Chris Beth leaned back and inhaled deeply. Once, while trying to sooth Vangie in later years, she had said bitterly of Hugo Stein in her growing skepticism, "He's no better, but maybe no worse, than the rest of humanity."

Well, she was wrong. That was before she had met such people as these who surrounded her now. No need to fake gratitude any longer! It welled up inside and there came an unfamiliar urge to express it in a way that went back farther than she could remember with any degree of clarity. But to *whom?* This beautiful Oregon Country? No, *for* it. Its inhabitants? No, for them, too.

The "thank you" Chris Beth sent out through the purpling dusk was directed at nobody in particular—or so she thought. But its utterance brought a strange tranquility to her heart.

9

Graveyard Shack

Joe came on Tuesday to say that Nate Goldsmith had postponed his trip to the store for two weeks. "As well as the opening of school," he concluded. "Corn and pumpkins are still in the field. Apples to pick and potatoes to harvest."

"But the exam?" Inwardly Chris Beth was thinking about mailing the brooch. Also, she *must* get a letter off to Mama. There had been no communication since she had posted a letter home at Redding. In it she had given a glowing account of the trip. Mama never liked bad news. Years of shielding her had created a pattern. Anyway, friends would be asking, *and I'll give their tongues no chance to wag.* Better a girl in her position be called fickle over the broken engagement than jilted! And better yet if she could carry off this "great adventure" aura she had woven so cleverly before coming West.

Joe smiled and responded to her question. "Nate will pick up papers and proctor the test in due time. But you passed *his* examination last week. He's a stickler on this commitment business. Which reminds me—he made mention of church."

Chris Beth nodded, wondering what was expected of her.

"Would you like me to pick you up S-Sunday? Any day could be our last for using the arbor before the rains s-set in."

"That would be nice," Chris Beth murmured. Actually, she felt a need to sort things out. Church hadn't been a part of her plans here. Of course, she *had* "committed" herself. But something else troubled her, too. Remembering the harmless little incident coming back from the Goldsmith house warned that she was less immune to love than she had thought. Memory of Joe's hand, warm through her thin blouse, brought a blush. And his slight stammer said he was self-conscious in her presence again.

Abruptly, Joe changed the subject. "Will you be needing supplies for school?"

Chris Beth had given the matter no thought. "Am I to furnish them?" she asked.

"Oh, the youngsters bring their own. I meant personal things—boots and other rainwear. You know, umbrella and a slicker."

She glanced at Joe's face. No, he wasn't teasing. "Are they essential?" Both of them looked at her pearl-button shoes.

This time he laughed. " 'Fraid so. Sometimes the general store stocks them. Mostly, people order from the catalogue, or else hope the backpack peddler happens to have a pair that fits!"

"Is there *nowhere* to shop?" This was incredulous.

"Well, there's Portland—a two-day trip. Each way."

Talk of isolation! Well, Mama had said it was a wilderness. Little did she know what it was like to live in one, though!

As it turned out, the arrangement never materialized. On the following Saturday Joe dropped by Turn-Around Inn to say he would be in town several days.

Town?

Well, the general store. Upstairs had some business offices...Doc Dullus. Blacksmith shop in shed next door. Smithy sometimes pulled teeth.

Mercy! Did Joe have a toothache?

"Nothing like that," Joe smiled. "The examining board—"

Mrs. Malone called, "Refreshments!" before Chris Beth could decide if it were proper to ask what the board was or what it had to do with Joe.

Over cinnamon rolls and coffee, Mrs. Malone asked about Joe's "tests" as she added to a list of staples she wanted him to pick up at the general store.

"I'm prepared," he said, slowly, "except f-for—" he stopped in embarrassment. Chris Beth made a mental note to ask Mrs. Malone what tests Joe was taking and why he was embarrassed.

"Is there something I can do for you, Miss Kelly?"

I must tell him to use my first name, except in front of the children, she thought. He's Joe to me and—"Miss Kelly?"

"Sorry," Chris Beth mumbled. "Yes, yes, there is, please. I'd like you to mail something." Excusing herself, she went for the overdue letter to her mother.

"Anything more?" he asked when she handed it to him. Chris Beth hesitated. "No, I think not." She was still undecided how to handle the return of the brooch to Jonathan Blake.

On the front porch Joe paused. "Wilson offered to come for you Sunday."

Chris Beth's lips pursed for a "No!" But before it came, she remembered that the Malones needed no additional passengers. Seven of them, plus O'Higgin (she was sure), made a wagonload. Oh, not to forget the dog. "Wolf always goes," Andy had said, "just in case." She hadn't cared to know of what!

"Miss Kelly," Joe prompted again.

"That would be nice," she murmured, careful to use the same words and exact tone as when she had accepted his own invitation. Then, as an afterthought, she added, "Call me Chris Beth. Aren't we friends?"

"Indeed we are that!" Joe mounted Dobbin and waved goodbye.

Well, out of the frying pan and into the fire. Chris Beth almost laughed aloud when she caught Mrs. Malone's unique speech entering into her own thinking. Anyway, the analogy best described the trip to the brush arbor. She would not be alone with Joe, after all. But she would be alone with that unnerving Wilson North...

Nothing about Wilson should have surprised her, but the wide-tired, two-wheeled cart in which he called for her on Sunday did! The single seat was upholstered in carmine stripes. So was the enormous umbrella which he had opened above it. How vulgar!

And what on earth occupied most of the seat? Wilson's command answered the question. "Wait here, Esau!" "Esau," whose canine coat put Wolf's to shame, showed no intention of leaving his throne. Back home they would be the laughingstock!

Chris Beth jabbed a hatpin through the wire frame of her plumed hat. Maybe the monstrous animal would "tree" the feather, thinking it was a bird. Remembering Wolf's antics last night, which had sent the 'possum scurrying up the backyard cedar, made her laugh again. Or maybe it was Wilson North, his outlandish vehicle, or the creature he called "Esau"!

Traces of laughter lingered when Wilson knocked, called "Open Sesame!" and entered.

"Well, now, *that's* a pretty sight, *you* laughing!" But his sweeping glance from the velvet hat, to the high-button shoes said Wilson North appreciated more than her smile. She straightened her face primly. Then, in strange contradiction, she felt unexpectedly glad that she had left the lace bertha on the blue wool for the Sunday service.

"Charlie Horse" (Chris Beth giggled at that name, too) was impatient to be off. Once she was wedged between the right rail and Esau, who refused to budge, the black pony shot forward.

The dog, thank goodness, looked straight ahead. To Chris Beth's surprise, the cart balanced perfectly for easy riding. She found herself almost lighthearted as they entered the stretch of woods leading past the Goldsmith place.

"Easy, Boy!" Wilson reined in as the trail narrowed. Chris Beth again drank in the beauty of the brilliant leaves. She remembered then that the man beside her was a botanist.

"What kind of trees?"

"Vine maple."

"Aren't you writing a book about trees?"

Wilson nodded but changed the subject. "Colorful, aren't they? Sort of the garden variety. See, there's cantaloupe orange." He pointed to a near-gold leaf.

The game caught her imagination. "Beet red," she suggested of a scarlet leaf, realizing that her comparison was trite.

"Watermelon, then?" They both burst into laughter. Strange, she thought, how she had laughed with both men in this same enchanted place. Only there was a difference she would have been unable to explain.

Abruptly Wilson consulted his pocket watch. "Time to drop by for a squint at the Graveyard shack before the singing begins if we step along."

"The what?"

"Place you're considering as a home, so they tell me."

"Oh, the cabin. Is it really called *that?*"

"*That's* what it is."

Chris Beth stole a look at the clean-shaven face above the starched collar—handsome, she had to admit, but not smiling. And something about that made her apprehensive.

"Let's go, Charlie Horse!" At Wilson's words, the pony backed his ears and picked up speed. *It's like a colored kaleidoscope,* Chris Beth thought, *and we're inside. Alone!*

10

Strange Visitor

The stretch of bright woods ended abruptly. A large, two-story house, fashioned much like the southern mansions of Chris Beth's youth, sprang out of nowhere. There was something both inviting and forbidding about the small paned windows that peered like a thousand eyes from the white exterior. Smoke climbed lazily from what appeared to be an upstairs fireplace. Sun touched the shake roof, but the rest of the house blended into the shady vale of the background. Somewhere a pheasant crowed.

"I call it home," Wilson North said with mock humility.

"It's beautiful," Chris Beth breathed. "But do you live here all alone?"

At his curt "No," she regretted asking. *He always makes me feel in the wrong,* she thought. *I'll keep my curiosity to myself.*

As if to forestall any further questions, Wilson pointed. "Over there's Joe's place."

Straining against the shadows, Chris Beth's eyes picked out the outline of the cabin that Joseph Craig had pointed out on their way to the Malones that first day. Was that only three weeks ago? It seemed a lifetime.

The cabin was close, as settlers measured distance, but a wide stream lay between the two houses.

"Graveyard Creek," Wilson explained. "Looks innocent now, but it can play havoc when Chinook winds melt the snowpack."

"How do you cross these creeks? And," she remembered, "doesn't the river run almost all the way around Turn-Around Inn?"

Wilson nodded. "Joe and I just fell a fir and drop it across the creek. Floods wash them away every year, which is just as well. The foot-logs get mossy and slippery anyway. Once," he laughed remembering, "the parson and his fine lady fell in the creek here!"

Chris Beth laughed with him. He continued, "My mother insisted that a board be nailed atop after that and a wire stretched for a handhold."

The slim, stout log spanning Graveyard Creek was arrowstraight. It looked like it would last forever. The floods must pack a wallop. No wonder settlers dreaded the winter.

Wilson had slowed the horse to a walk. "As to crossing the river, mostly people ford when the water's high."

Ford?

He explained about wading horses across and floating the wagon bed. *Well!* It was becoming clear why Joe thought she would be needing boots!

For some time Chris Beth had been conscious of a distant roar. As the cart moved into the woods again, the noise was closer.

"Graveyard Falls." Wilson raised his voice as the roar became near-deafening. "About half a mile upstream! Furnishes power for the grist mill—mine and Joe's. We supply settlers—and more."

How many more surprises did these two enterprising young men have in store, for goodness' sake?

"Grist—like for flour and meal?" Chris Beth supposed the question sounded silly and citified. And, sure enough, it was just the "grist" Wilson North needed for his humor to feed upon.

"Ah, yes." He faked a sigh. "Notice how our feet turn inward? That's from tramping flour into barrels for export. And the meal—"

Charlie Horse interrupted his sentence by stopping at a pole gate. They had reached a rail fence which surrounded a building of sorts. At least, a rusty tin roof showed above it.

"Good boy! Well," Wilson alighted and offered his hand "Welcome to Graveyard Shack." She accepted his hand and stepped down.

He opened the gate and Chris Beth stepped through—then stopped dead in her tracks, aghast at what she saw. Surely this crude lean-to could not be the "cabin" that Nate Goldsmith had mentioned. Why, it offered less protection than the temporary quarters occupied by miners she had seen in California. And they were men! Small wonder Joe hadn't been in a hurry to bring her to such a place.

Aware that Wilson North was watching, Chris Beth mustered as much dignity as possible, picked up her wool skirt, and stepped through the dried thistles. The one-room shanty slanted crazily as if to meet her. Involuntarily she stepped back.

"There's no window," was all she could gasp.

"'No window,' she says," Wilson mused, then—as if inspired—"but oh, what a view! Creek from the front and the graveyard from the back—if it had a back door."

Chris Beth jumped at a strange flapping noise coming from the shack.

"Not to worry!" Wilson soothed. "Not in daylight hours, that is. It's night when the strange visitor comes. He—"

"He who?" Chris Beth realized that her eyes must be round with fear. She was past caring about Wilson's silly banter aimed at her.

"Nobody knows for sure—not even if he's white or Indian. Both, they say, are buried here. He comes to claim them."

He's poking fun at me, she reasoned, *like always. The noise is coming from the piece of canvas serving as a door.* Of course, it had been his wild tales…and her imagination…like Brom Bones and Ichabod Crane.

But it was no use. She was unable to regain her composure. A wild laugh rose in her throat. Escape was all that mattered.

"Miss Kelly." There was sudden concern in Wilson North's voice. "Chris Beth—"

"Please—please," she pled through stiff lips, "take me away."

He touched her elbow, but she tore away and climbed frantically into the cart.

Even Charlie Horse seemed strangely subdued. Like "Gun Powder," she thought, remembering the one-eyed nag in *The Legend of Sleepy Hollow.*

"Chris Beth, listen to me. Please do."

When Wilson spoke, Chris Beth was sure he spoke softly, but his voice had a ghostly ring in the silence of the woods. Charlie Horse picked up speed, and it was comforting to note that the cart rolled swiftly toward another clearing once his riders were aboard. The hammering of her heart was easing, but Chris Beth dared not risk her voice.

"I'm sorry. I truly am." Wilson's voice said that he was unaccustomed to apologizing. *That light touch is a coverup,* she thought. *He's been hurt—like me.* Fear gave way to surprise.

"I understand," Chris Beth spoke slowly. Yes, she understood more than the graveyard incident—or thought she did. For she was beginning to understand the man, and maybe herself.

But she did not understand his next words. "Joe and me, and the others, had to show you it's impossible for a fine lady like you to live there. I personally will see to that!" *He* would see to it! What propriety did Wilson North have?

But for the first time Chris Beth did not meet his challenge. Maybe *she* was the strange visitor in this new land.

11

Raisin' Praise

It was a relief to feel warm sunshine in her face. This is the *real* world, she said to herself, once they reached the clearing. The other was a dream. But, deep inside, Chris Beth knew that both worlds were a part of this Western frontier. And here one must live in them both, or perish.

"Feeling better?"

Chris Beth answered Wilson with a nod. It was good to feast her eyes on the now-golden meadows, dotted with livestock, like "the cattle on a thousand hills." Now *that* was familiar.

Before she could think more about the source, Wilson pointed ahead. "Mount Hood," he said.

And there to the east loomed the magnificent mountain she had seen in geography books. The snow-capped peak seemed to finger into the very sky, but the base of the mountain looked deceptively near. Vision on this kind of day reached into infinity.

"It's unbelievable," she breathed deeply. As usual, the beauty of this land tricked her into forgetting the problems at hand. "Mr. North—"

"Wilson."

"Wilson—do you realize I didn't even see the school."

"I realize."

The school…a place to live…returning the brooch…the state

board exam…even, she thought wryly, a pair of boots! But somehow it didn't matter right now. Those were tomorrow's problems.

Charlie Horse's ears stood suddenly alert. Somewhere he had heard a whinny from another of his kind. And, sure enough, just over the horizon Chris Beth caught sight of the beautiful black taffeta bonnet belonging to Mollie Malone. She had worked until the lamps were out of oil last night trying to get the last of the pink rosettes embroidered around the ruffle. In her lap sat little Jimmy John. And close beside them, Chris Beth recognized the red pom pom on top of O'Higgin's Scottish-plaid tam o'shanter.

"Top o' the mornin'!" O'Higgin called when Chris Beth and Wilson were within hearing distance. His cheeks were as bright as his woolen cap. *He's harboring some sort of exciting secret,* Chris Beth decided, and wondered what it was that set the man aglow.

There was a happy babble of children's voices at the intersection. Wolf and Esau eyed each other suspiciously but kept their seats. Greetings over, Wilson let Charlie Horse have free rein, and the cart wheeled away from the loaded wagon.

The road wound in and out of heavily wooded areas and past occasional clearings made for erecting cabins and cultivating. The ground must be very fertile to yield such gardens. Lush pumpkin vines trailed through corn rows; pausing only long enough to dump their golden fruits in any lap they could find.

"It looks so rich."

"Rich enough to mine," Wilson told her. "All virgin soil, you know, sometimes as much as three or four feet down. It's a land with a future, all right."

She could see that. Someday the railroads would come on through. The waterways would be developed. More and more settlers would come and towns would spring up.

Wilson broke into her dream to point out the young orchards. "Prunes, peaches—and see the apples?"

No store back home ever saw the like, she was sure. Huge, rosy, and polished, they glistened in the sun. And the ground beneath the trees was carpeted with fallen, wine-scented fruit! Her mouth watered. Wilson saw and laughed. "There'll be no breaking of the commandments," he cautioned, "until after church!"

Yes, the Oregon Country was a land of promise—for some. Chris Beth wondered what it held for her. But for right now this day was one of Mrs. Malone's "rainbows in between" life's dark days and its bright.

Chris Beth heard the sound of laughter mingled with excited voices of children before she saw the arbor. Up a little hill, a sudden dip in the road, and there it was! Where on earth had all the wagons and buggies, come from? From miles around, Wilson told her. "And just wait till you see the picnic baskets and the appetites! Be lucky if we get a chicken neck!"

By the time the men watered the horses and tethered them to trees, Mrs. Malone had her flock "presentable" with Lola Ann's help. Amelia's sash was retied. Harmony's hair ribbon was straightened. "And, Chris Beth—Miss Kelly—will you unsnarl Andy's shoelaces?" Chris Beth was both amused and touched by the matter-of-fact way this woman filled the shoes of the dead mother's children. And the children obviously adored their stepmother. Even now little Jimmy John was reaching dimpled hands to show her that his cowlick was standing up again. Mrs. Malone grabbed an embroidered handkerchief, spit on it, and pushed back the unruly lock. *She's all women rolled into one,* Chris Beth thought, and was surprised to realize that she envied the other woman a bit.

As Chris Beth brushed her skirt free of possible dust and made sure the plume on her hat was still intact, she noticed a sudden hush about her. "Hurry, they're about to begin," O'Higgin whispered.

The group moved quickly to join the assembled worshipers. There was total silence as they stepped beneath the split-rail frame roofed with fir boughs, dry and brittle but sweet-smelling in the near-noon sun. Their footsteps made no sound on the dirt floors. All heads were bowed.

Chris Beth ventured a look around. A crude pulpit stood in front of the congregation (who were seated on split logs), and beside the pulpit was a tin bucket. It contained water, she supposed, since there was a dipper inside. Primitive though it was, there was a certain warmth—something missing in the straight, hard pews back home

Involuntarily, her mind went back to the stiffly ritualistic services that her "God-fearing" stepfather had forced her mother, Vangie, and herself to sit through. Certainly the speakers had been eloquent, if selective, in their long, solemn sermons, which always gave Mama a headache and left Chris Beth and Vangie scared and depressed The men were well-educated scholars who literally "scared hell *out* of the parishioners," she had dared tell her "Father Stein" once. She winced at the memory of quinine he had forced under her tongue...but these people, uneducated though they were, were more enlightened. They seemed to be freed of the restraints of fear and superstition. It should have been the other way around!

Chris Beth came out of her reverie. A man—why, it was Nate Goldsmith!—rose to stand behind the pulpit. Though almost obscured from view, Nate's voice rose powerfully. "The Lord bless you, one and all," he began. "Now, folks, I am sorry to be tellin' you that there's no big preach today. The circuit rider cain't come till maybe Thanksgiving, at which time we be meetin' at Turn-Around Inn." His eyes consulted Mrs. Malone. She nodded and he continued: "But there's a heap of food, judgin' by the way my old woman's been cookin'." He paused, and little snickers of appreciation rippled through the crowd. "And meantime, we'll be raisin' praise!"

At his signal, O'Higgin stepped forward, lifted his hand, lowered it ceremoniously, and the group burst into song. "Praise God from whom all blessings flow!"

After that, with O'Higgin's booming Irish voice in the lead, the group sang hymn after hymn. "Who has a selection?" he would ask.

"Bringin' in the Sheaves!"..."Ole Rugged Cross" "Amazin' Grace"..."Rescue the Perishin'..." "When We All Git to Heaven!" One member after another requested.

The crowd seemed lost in emotion as their words tumbled out in song without the aid of a piano or organ to accompany their singing. Chris Beth had never heard "pure song" before. So many of the lyrics had been drowned out by robed choruses and heavy-footed organists.

She listened with sad-sweet appreciation to the velvety bass melting gently into tenor—the plaintive minor keys rising to melodious major key. The very arbor seemed to tremble with praise raised to a God whom her stepfather had never met.

When a small lad suggested "Blessed Assurance," Chris Beth listened carefully to the words, which she was unsure she had heard before:

> Blessed assurance, Jesus is mine!
> O what a foretaste of glory divine!
> Heir of salvation, purchase of God,
> Born of His Spirit, washed in His blood...

O'Higgin lifted his hand. The singing stopped. "'I will sing praises unto my God while I have any being,'" he declared. "Psalm 146:2."

As others quoted favorite passages of Scripture, Chris Beth listened, carefully taking note that all the verses spoke of joy, love, and praise.

And the final quotation struck home: "'Lord, I believe; help thou mine unbelief.' Mark 9:24."

Something stirred within her—something sweet and good, that went beyond her stepfather's coming into her life. She was sorry when the crowd rose to sing "Till We Meet Again."

12

A Family of Friends

People came forward eagerly to meet "the new teacher," but Nate Goldsmith pushed his way ahead of the group to pump her hand. "Picked 'er myself, I did," he said proudly. "Now, men, she's single and bound to stay thata way. But you women are to welcome 'er, hear?"

One by one, Nate presented Chris Beth to the Smiths (old timers, he said), Martins ("kinda new, but learnin'"), Beltrans ("Basque folks, who raise wooly critters"—sheep, she supposed), and then Chris Beth lost track of the names. She noticed, however, that the board member paused significantly when he introduced the Solomons. "Him and the missus operate the general store."

Abe Solomon, short of stature and breath, acknowledged the introduction and bumped into his wife, immediately behind him, in his hurry to get away. Mrs. Solomon, on the other hand, took her own good time in assessing Chris Beth. "I suppose you know about the perils of being alone out here—no place to live and all?"

Chris Beth knew, only too well!

"Rainy weather and need of proper apparel?"

That, too—as well as Indians, wild animals, and no mail service.

"Though men outnumber women, finding a man whose intentions are pure is like hoping a peddler will come along with a good supply of darning needles!"

Well, of all the nerve! Chris Beth was tempted to walk away, but Mrs. Solomon seemed to sense that. "This is my daughter, Maggie."

With a rustle of taffeta, Maggie, who appeared to be about Chris Beth's own age, stepped from behind her mother. Maggie's lips, which looked suspiciously like she had rouged them, smiled. But her green-grape eyes did not. "So you've met Wilson North."

Chris Beth ignored the impertinent remark and forced herself to smile. "I hope we'll be friends, Maggie."

Maggie did not return her smile. "Warning—he's not the marryin' kind!"

So that's what put the burr under her mother's saddle! Something of the old spirit flared up. "Then I shall make it a point to see a lot of him," she said pertly. "I'm not the marrying kind either!"

When Chris Beth felt a hand at her elbow, she turned to face Wilson North. She flushed, wondering how much he had heard.

Later, Mrs. Malone asked how she had fared with the Solomons.

"I don't think they appreciate my presence in the settlement," Chris Beth told her. "Not the ladies, anyway."

Mrs. Malone laughed heartily. "Of course not! You're too pretty. Bertie Solomon's been tryin' to marry Maggie off to Wilson or Joe since her bornin' day."

Chris Beth wondered whether to reveal her little set-to with Maggie and decided against it. She wanted to give nobody the false impression that men entered into her planning—now or ever.

"They mean well, though." Mrs. Malone went on to explain the Solomons. "Bertie's just ambitious for that girl. Come an emergency here in the settlement and they put aside such trifles."

Her impression of the others?

Oh, very favorable, Chris Beth assured Mrs. Malone truthfully.

"Good folks—all of 'em. We're *family* here, a family of friends. But," Mrs. Malone sighed, "just like any other family, we're sometimes happy and peaceful and sometimes jealous like."

Well put, Chris Beth thought. She herself had been able to handle a baby sister—be overjoyed by her presence, in fact. But she remembered the all-too-frequent jealousies on Vangie's part.

"So I'd just forget Bertie's petty ways. Today she looked like she'd been samplin' my sauerkraut. Next time it's apt to be my quince honey." Mrs. Malone paused. "Somethin' else wrong?"

Chris Beth related the Graveyard Shack incident.

Mrs. Malone nodded understandingly but said nothing. Chris Beth volunteered, "I just wish I knew what to do about a place to stay. It seems so hopeless."

"Put your hope in the Lord!" Mrs. Malone replied. "Didn't I say you're among a family of friends?"

13

Inventory

October's blush deepened. Soon it would be November and time for school to open. The Malones, aided by O'Higgin, had been busily preparing for winter. Fortunately, the rains had held their distance, so corn was in shocks, pumpkins were piled up ready for storing in the hay, and potatoes were in the root cellar. Chris Beth had insisted on helping and, although she stained her hands and broke her nails to the quick, she found something decidedly healing about touching the rich, raw earth.

Mrs. Malone, busy with putting up green tomato mincemeat, pickling, and canning the last of the late pears, welcomed her help in the kitchen. The children, delighted with her ability to make ginger-bread custard pies, redoubled their efforts to help "Miss Mollie" when promised seconds on dessert.

But helping was not enough on Chris Beth's part. She knew that her being at Turn-Around Inn was an added burden. When the old house sighed and settled down comfortably for the night, she tried to do the same thing. But sometimes sleep was slow in coming. She thought about Mama and Vangie and wondered how they were. She thought about Indian summer back home and a sort of regional homesickness enveloped her. She thought about the heartbreak of her broken engagement...

But somehow through it all she felt the pain lessening to the point that she was able to go about the business of taking and passing her exam when Nate brought it to her, unpacking the necessary school supplies she had brought along, and making arrangements to accept Joe's invitation to see the school next Wednesday. School would start the following Monday. Now if only she could find a place to stay!

It seemed incredibly dark when Chris Beth awakened on Wednesday morning. True, the days were shortening in preparation for the deep sleep of winter. But the darkness seemed too sudden. Before rolling up the feather bed, she opened the brocade drape and checked the sky from the front-room window. The sky was banked with dark clouds, and there was an eerie stillness that portends a storm no matter where one lives. Would Joe be coming when the skies looked like this?

Mrs. Malone's coffee was bracing, but Chris Beth was unable to shake off a sense of depression in keeping with the weather. Mrs. Malone was packing ham sandwiches made with leftovers from "salting down the pork" into a small picnic basket. She paused to note that the "needed moisture to green up the meadows" was overdue.

"But should we go to the school on a rainy day?"

"If you failed to show up on rainy days hereabouts, my child, our little ones would never learn to read!"

Joe, too, took the change of weather in stride. She noticed that he had thrown slickers in the back of the buggy, but he seemed almost unaware that a fine mist—typical of the area, she was to learn—had begun to fall. He seemed cheerful, almost exuberant, as he moved a container of garden-spearmint tea from underfoot. She climbed quickly into the buggy, before he could assist her. She wondered about his tests. Maybe passing explained his mood. But a certain reserve kept her from asking what might be construed as a personal question.

Chris Beth was relieved to see that, although the school was only a stone's throw from Graveyard Creek and the cemetery itself, the hateful shack was down-creek just enough to be out of view. The school building, made of split logs, looked a little more inviting than the "cabin."

"An acre of donated ground for students to romp on," Joe pointed out. And then they went inside.

To Chris Beth's amazement, there was no floor! Suddenly she wished she had failed the teacher's exam after all. "Does the roof leak?" she asked weakly.

"Some," Joe admitted, "but the men plan to reshake it this winter when there's less field work, and maybe even floor the room."

And chink up the cracks, too, she thought. Or was that the settlers' idea of natural ventilation?

"Oh, and Nate told me to give you this," Joe said, reaching into the pocket of his jacket. "Inventory."

Bravely accepting the scribbled list, Chris Beth read with increasing disbelief: "One broom (most new), one box chalk (part used last year), gallon water bucket (no leaks), one dipper (new!), and ten chords of green wood (bought by school board to keep within said budget)." *This was the year's equipment?*

A quick survey of the four walls showed a four-year-old calendar, a faded flag, and a book-lined shelf. She hurriedly examined the titles, laying them aside one by one in despair. "Oh, Joe, have you seen these?"

Joe hadn't, but as he looked, he too laid them aside after reading aloud, *"Medical Science, Veterinary Practices, Navigation, Common Works on Engineering…*

"For my chart class? Why, the eighth-graders can't handle them!"

Joe agreed. And without warning they both burst into laughter. When finally Joe was in control of himself he explained, "Belonged to some professor who came over the Applegate Trail, as I recall. The children bring some things, I understand."

"And I brought some—" She jumped. "What was that?"

A loud yell had pierced the silence around them. And out of the shrouds of mist the figure of a boy about 12 emerged.

"It's Elmer, one of the Goldsmith boys," Joe decided.

Elmer reached the door too winded to speak. Mutely, he handed a letter to Chris Beth.

And mutely she read the devastating contents.

14

Impossible Request

The five or so miles back to Turn-Around seemed an eternity. At last the old inn's welcome outline loomed ahead. The glory of the woods faded without the sunshine. Shawls of fog wrapped the trees, causing Chris Beth to wonder if ambush awaited her and Joe somewhere in the damp quiet. She needed to be home to think.

If Joseph Craig noticed that she too was silent like the trees, he gave no indication. She had been careful since their first ride through the secluded stretch of woods that the small intimate touching of the two of them not be misleading. She found herself desperately anxious that his hand on her shoulder and her responsiveness had not promised anything further. She wouldn't have thought herself capable of responding at all. Well, it wouldn't happen again. It was dreadful to remember that she had forgotten herself…but most likely Joe had forgotten it. He seemed almost formal in his politeness. She could stop worrying.

But silence today had nothing to do with the incident. Chris Beth reached into her satchel, hoping that the fateful letter had been a bad dream like some of the others she had had. But the letter crackled to her touch, unrolling slightly as if to free itself from the tight wad she had made and to force her to read in full what she had read only in part. *I'll never read it,* she told herself fiercely. *If I do, I'll die again and that's not possible!*

The awful truth, of course, was that what she *had* read stamped itself indelibly in her memory. Nothing would erase it. Trying would only smear it and make it spread, smudging the new page of life she had turned over in the settlement.

Oh, Mama, couldn't you just once have thought of something—anything—instead of putting it on my shoulders? In an effort to stave off making a decision concerning the impossible request, Chris Beth turned her thoughts to the mother-daughter relationship she wished her mother and she could have had. How nice it would have been to feel protected as a child, and then take her broken heart to Mama when Jon broke the engagement. But Mama remained forever the child. The truth was that Vangie was the favorite one—until now! Now Mama wouldn't even assume responsibility for helping Vangie. Poor Vangie... Thinking of her sister, brought fragments of the letter back, dimly at first and then with startling clarity.

> My dear Christen Elizabeth:
>
> By now you are settled, and that's good, for there are terrible problems at home. Your father is most distraught—poor man—and I have been not at all well. This is much more than a mother should be called upon to bear—one daughter leaving me alone to face friends with our recent embarrassment and running away to chase a dream. But now you must put aside all selfishness and come to the aid of the family.

As she stood in the one-room school building, desperately wishing she need read no further, Chris Beth was aware of Joe's eyes on her face. She turned away, afraid of what her eyes might reveal. Whatever had to be handled was her problem. Mama would see to that! With dread, she returned to the letter but could not avoid skipping some lines.

> Your sister has fallen into disgrace! Jonathan Her father has disowned her...nobody to turn to...my only comfort being

that Evangeline will find a place with you…families have
to rally in such circumstances…nobody here need know…
she'll be able to hide her shame….

*Oh, Mama, it's not just her father who disowned your daughter.
You did too!* That's when Chris Beth wadded the letter into a ball,
consumed by her emotions. What was it she felt? *Hatred,* of course,
for the zealot, "Father Stein"! *Disgust* with her helpless mother—
and guilt for feeling that way. *Shock,* yes, that Vangie, little Vangie,
was somehow caught in such an unbelievable circumstance. In
their circle, no "nice girl" gave birth out of wedlock. Illegitimacy
occurred only among "trash." "Brier patch babies," they were called,
and Chris Beth remembered with shame that she and her friends
had giggled behind their fans about such goings-on. She felt a growing distrust, too. This only confirmed what she had learned from
Jon—a man was not to be trusted. But, above all else, Chris Beth
felt a gnawing fear—fear such as she had never known before. It
was a writhing, living thing that clutched her heart and squeezed
it dry.

It had taken all the small legacy her own father had left for her to
complete her teacher training and buy the train and stagecoach tickets
to the Oregon Country. Vangie would have no money if the devilish
man had kicked her out of their mother's home. She fought down a
new fury at the thought. That house belonged to her own father. Her
stepfather had no right…but she must not dwell on that.

If only she could get word to Vangie not to come. On second
thought, where would her younger sister go if she rejected her?

Chris Beth was unaware that she had groaned until Joe said softly,
"Let me help. I'm your friend, you know."

She realized then that Dobbin had stopped in front of Turn-
Around Inn. "You can't help," she whispered through achingly-tight
lips. "Nobody can." And sobbing she ran past Mrs. Malone and the
wide-eyed Malone children who had waited for her return on the
wide porch, eager to hear all about the new school year.

Inside, the first fire of the season crackled cheerfully in the fireplace. Fiercely, Chris Beth threw the wadded letter into it. Tongues of flame leaped up the chimney, taking with them the unread news that her sister already was on her way West.

15

Spreading the News

Emptily, as if in a sleep-induced dream, Chris Beth moved through the remainder of the week. Once again, she realized that the unthinkable is possible. One *could* die more than once—and then go on living. Maybe she had been "reborn" as in the Scriptures, as some of the settlers had quoted at the brush-arbor service. She wondered vaguely if one could be reborn a little each day. All this she was thinking in some distant corner of her mind as she counted with dismay the small sum of cash she had and wondered if it would cover the bare essentials for herself. If she had the nine lives the Malone children claimed for "Ambrose," the roving yellow tomcat, who would hand her crumbs like his? And for Vangie, too? But each time such terrifying thoughts invaded her sleepwalking, Chris Beth pushed them from her conscious mind. They would only bring panic, depression…bad dreams…hysteria.

"Get a list ready. We're goin' school-shoppin' come Thursday!" Mrs. Malone's announcement dispensed with a need for roll-calling. *All* were going. And no questions. So life went on.

The general store was better-equipped than Chris Beth would have supposed. The walls were lined with ropes, harness, pitchforks, twine, fly paper, and snakebite cures. Granite pots and pans were heaped on a long counter, and beside them picks and shovels. There were giant bins of sugar and coffee beans ready for grinding. Laces, buttons, garter-webbing, and corset stays on the notion counter were reassuring. She looked further.

Crudely-printed signs (lettered from tar, judging from their odor) boasted of supplies for MINERS, PROSPECTORS, FARMERS, LUMBERJACKS, and MILADY'S SECRET NEEDS.

Nothing secret about the display!

There was no fire in the pot-bellied stove, but men gathered around it anyway. As they whittled or played checkers, they talked of "harvestin'"and "'lection year." Over all, there was an overpowering smell of camphor, sassafras, and something Chris Beth could describe only as a "new-merchandise scent," even though most of it looked "old enough to vote," Mrs. Malone had warned on their trip in from the settlement. The store should have looked dismal, but instead there was a warm, friendly atmosphere.

O'Higgin hurried to the "Blasting Counter," with the boys at his heels. Mrs. Malone propelled the girls to the dry goods department, where Mrs. Solomon presided.

Maggie stepped from behind shipping boxes without greeting.

"I need boots—" Chris Beth began.

"This way."

As Chris Beth struggled into and out of boots in an effort to find a pair remotely close to her size, Maggie said abruptly, "Did Elmer Goldsmith deliver your letter in proper shape?"

Why, yes, thank you.

Hoped it wasn't bad news.

Well—no!

She would be able to *stay* here then?

Oh, yes indeed! As a matter of fact her sister would be joining her soon.

Chris Beth could have bitten off her tongue. At the same time she secretly took satisfaction in the look of undisguised shock in the other girl's eyes. *Another Southern belle in the settlement,* it plainly said, *when one's too many!*

Mrs. Malone joined them. "And we'll all be welcomin' her, won't we, Maggie?"

The girl nodded sullenly as she accepted money for the boots and Chris Beth's few other purchases.

How much does Mrs. Malone know? Chris Beth wondered. It didn't matter. Neither did she care how Mrs. Malone had come to know at all. What mattered was to have the news out in the open. She and the older woman exchanged a look of understanding. How better to spread the news than through the spiteful Maggie? Now that it was told, Chris Beth felt as if a boulder had been removed from her chest. She could breathe. And didn't that mean living?

On the way out, Mrs. Malone paused to look at an enormous heart-shaped box. Just below the red velvet rose that decorated the lid, assorted chocolates showed invitingly through the cellophane window—round and plump, topped with nuts and dried fruits.

Unaware that anybody watched, Mrs. Malone reached out and touched the bow, then jerked her hand away guiltily. But Chris Beth had seen a sense of longing in the woman's eyes. O'Higgin had seen it too, apparently.

"Mighty pretty, eh, Miss Mollie?" he said, moving to her side.

"Mighty frivolous, if you ask me!"

Somehow Chris Beth knew that Mrs. Malone had never eaten a chocolate candy. And something in that knowledge made her sad.

The trip back to Turn-Around Inn was festive. The children were exuberant over the bolts of calico that Mrs. Malone had bought. Chris Beth felt relieved to have spoken out. And O'Higgin made it complete; "Horehound for all of ye—though mighty frivolous it be!" His mischievous blue eyes rolled toward Mrs. Malone with the announcement. Chris Beth saw Andy count the three candies which were his portion as a king would count his treasures. Then, swallowing hard, he handed one to Wolf. She suddenly wished with all her heart that the whole world knew of the sharing and caring that went on here in this so-called "wilderness." It seemed only natural that she should quietly slip one of her own pieces of horehound into the little boy's pocket.

16

Blessed Assurance

On Saturday, after helping Mrs. Malone with the baking, Chris Beth asked Ned to take her to the school. The skies had cleared and the building looked, if not brighter, at least less dismal. Ned swept the bare floor, straightened the lines of double desks (logs, really, with rough board tables as desk tops), and wiped away the summer's dust. Chris Beth suggested that the boy lay a fire in the big wood stove while she "decorated."

"Never saw it look so purty," Ned said after she had made bouquets of colored leaves and Oregon grapes. "Can I help more?"

"Yes—if you have a pocket knife, cut out the letters for 'WEL-COME BACK.'" She handed him scraps of wrapping paper.

Ned did a fine job with making the letters, but when it came to arranging them, he was lost. Spelling was a problem with the boy, undoubtedly. *I'll have to find a way to help,* she thought.

On the way home, the two of them stopped to pick hazelnuts. "They're fun for roastin' over the fire," Ned promised for the evening ahead.

Sunday was clear and cold. A crisp wind blew in overnight, bringing what O'Higgin called "butcherin' weather." The beef he spoke of would be put up in jars. "First, we be eatin' all we can. Then what we can't eat, we can!"

Chris Beth smiled at his wit ("natural as his breathin'," Mrs.

Malone said of it), but something within her recoiled a little at his words. Winter was near, no doubt about it. She pressed her cheek against the pane of the front-room window and found it cold. A playful breeze was teasing speckled leaves from the oak in the yard and, although clouds were swept behind the mountains, a thin wisp of fog trailed warningly below the peaks. Something whispered frost.

"All aboard!" O'Higgin called from the wagon. Since Mrs. Malone had discovered that there was room for them all in the wagon if they "sorta scrooched up," she no longer felt in the way. Mrs. Malone laid a quilt over the children's feet. They promptly pulled it over their heads—with Wolf in the middle—and huddled together happily.

On the way to church, Chris Beth heard strange cries overhead. And then a familiar voice called out, "Canadian honkers!" Joe had joined the Malone wagon at the intersection. It was good to see him, she thought fleetingly, then returned her eyes to the sky. For a moment she envied the honkers—free creatures heading for the Southern climes. But their cries reminded her that they weren't so free after all. They too were escaping.

"Wilson," Joe interrupted her thoughts, "is giving Doc Dullus a hand over the weekend." He made no further explanation.

Would Joe ask her to ride with him? He did not.

The circuit rider, to the pleasure of the congregation, appeared unexpectedly for the worship service. He would be around for a few days, if "somebody can sort of board and keep me." Hands went up everywhere. This meant that they could be marrying off the young folks who had been waiting, have the man say the proper words for those who had suffered losses in their families, and enjoy news of what was going on in churches of the widely scattered communities.

Joe made a special effort to introduce Jonas Brown to Chris Beth, saying, "He's been a great help to me."

She wished she had been able to concentrate on the man's sermon. There should be a word of appreciation probably, but a polite curtsy was all she could manage. The look of surprise on the preacher's face told her that such acknowledgment of an introduction labeled her as a newcomer—maybe a foreigner! It was a little embarrassing and she regretted the formality that her own church had demanded back home.

Of course she had been expected to listen then, too, knowing that there would be a test on the sermon before her stepfather would allow her and Vangie to eat. Well, at least nobody was going to test her here, she hoped. Her mind had been on all the problems that lay ahead—problems which a demanding schedule had allowed her no time to think about until the quiet of today. The dreaded first day of school...where she could find lodging...what she and Vangie were to do.

When all the Malones were loaded into the wagon, O'Higgin offered a hand to the two women. "Trouble is when there be preachin', there be too little song."

The children heard and came from beneath the quilt. "Let's sing!" they all shouted at once.

The Irishman needed no coaxing. "Bringin' in the Sheaves," he announced, glancing at the burnished heads of late-ripening grain still in the fields.

As the group sang, Chris Beth joined in tentatively. It felt good to sing. It had been a long time, she realized suddenly, since she had sung. Mama had said she had a good voice—one of the few things she praised about her older daughter.

On and on they sang, the wagon wheels and horses' hooves seeming to keep time to their voices. Without realizing it, Chris Beth's own voice rose above the others. Her contralto seemed to drift up the mountain slopes and come back like an echo-chorus. The others had stopped singing—even O'Higgin—as she sang, "Blessed assurance, Jesus is mine!—" and stopped. The group, apparently thinking she had forgotten the words, picked up the refrain.

Actually, she needed to think. *Blessed assurance!* The phrase echoed again and again—this time against the slopes of her heart. And then she remembered one phrase of Scripture quoted at last Sunday's service: "Help thou my unbelief."

Gripping the arm rest of the spring seat, Chris Beth tasted the words and found them sweet.

Maybe—just maybe—the answers would come. This, after all, was a land of miracles.

17

First Day—
Its "Awful Glory"

November certainly put on its most somber garments for the first day, Chris Beth thought as she prepared herself to greet students of assorted sizes and colors who romped around the schoolyard. Earlier, dark clouds had bumped against the mountains, dumping scattered showers in the valley. Even now, fog was caught along the summit as if in silent watch. At least there would be no need to caution the children to wipe their shoes—not with a dirt floor! It would be damp, though. She bent stiffly to light the fire Ned had laid. She would probably be unable to walk tomorrow, she supposed, after her first ride astride a horse! O'Higgin had saddled the speckled pony for her.

A check of the hard-enameled watch pinned onto the lapel of her jacket said it was time to call the children inside. Chris Beth smoothed her dark hair and on impulse tucked a bronze chrysanthemum behind a heavy braid. Mrs. Malone had picked an enormous armload in preparation for what she called the "awful glory" of the first day!

"Just move in gentle like, knowin' water finds its own level," she had said with her usual insight. "Things'll right up before you know it. Nothing's ever so horrible—or so wonderful, as the case may be—as the first time around."

Chris Beth remembered and smiled as she pulled at the rope suspended to the giant outside "dinner bell."

Thirty-one children, eyeing her suspiciously, lined up and marched in wordlessly.

"Good morning, children!" she said brightly, hoping that her nervousness did not show. "I am your teacher."

Immediately a hand shot up. The little girl in a faded pinafore (one of the Goldsmith children, Chris believed) spoke in a voice as wee as herself. "Whatta we call you?"

"I am Miss Kelly."

The child nodded. "But whatta we *call* you?"

Confused, Chris Beth was about to repeat her surname when Ned Malone came to the rescue. Politely, lifting his hand for recognition, the boy said, "She means last year we called Miz Andrews Miss Lizzie."

First names then? But Miss Chris Beth was too cumbersome, let alone Miss Christen Elizabeth! Well, if that other Elizabeth could be Miss Lizzie, she could be.

"Call me Miss Chrissy," she smiled, liking the sound of it. One year's teaching in a city school was little help in a situation like this. Would they like to share a little of what they had done over the summer? The children stared at her blankly. Why, when we all did the same? their looks asked her. Well, then, they could introduce themselves and she would enter their names and grade level in the roll book.

The Malones, she knew, of course—one of them in seven of the eight grades. Ditto for the Goldsmiths, except that she would need to know their first names. Chris Beth recognized some of the other children from having met their parents at Sunday services, but there were strangers, too. She especially noticed a little almond-eyed boy who sat, with folded hands, apart from the others.

"Your name, please?" She made a point of smiling.

There was no reply.

"He can't talk," one of the children said.

A mute? But no! "He can too talk!" Another contradicted. "He just talks Chinaman!"

"Chinese," she corrected, and smiled again at the frightened child.

"I'll help," an especially bright-eyed child told Chris Beth. "I can speak it a little."

"Good." Chris Beth decided that the boy was probably as bright as his eyes. "I'll need his name—and yours."

"He's Wong—Wong Chu. They live in Railroad Camp way off somewhere. The others don't come to school." He inhaled importantly, "And me, I'm Wil, with one *l*. 'Young Wil' I'm called, or 'Willie.' Just write it down Willie Ames."

My! This one was a talker. Chris Beth smiled in amusement.

The job finished, Chris Beth felt a bit more at ease. But there was the matter of curriculum! With a sudden burst of inspiration, she announced that they would just start in where they had left off last year.

The children seemed satisfied. They rifled through sacks and satchels, bringing out papers—most of them dog-eared and dirty— and a few thin books, too old for titles to be readable. *These* were the supplies the board chairman had promised the children would bring?

But there were more surprises to come, none of them reassuring. "Oh, I brung a ball," one child announced, and promptly bounced it on the dirt floor. Six others, inspired by the boy's bravery, followed suit.

Startled, Chris Beth confiscated the balls and announced that they would become "school property." The children were awed to silence, and she knew she had won. Now to use the discipline constructively!

"We'll *all* enjoy ball games, *if* assignments are completed, *if* the floor is swept, *if* the wood is brought in, and *if*" she stressed, "we all behave ourselves!" *(Base hit!* she congratulated herself.)

"Now," she said matter-of-factly, "let's get down to business."

There would be a "division of labor."

A what?

Older students will help the younger ones.

Two recesses plus 45 minutes at noon.

But, Teacher, some has to go—

Well, yes, in emergencies.

"And there's a barrel stave outside for wiping their shoes on before coming back, if it's raining." That was young Wil again.

Most of the children had slates—a few of them new, but mostly broken pieces. One child drew out a shingle that someone had worked very hard to smooth with a jackknife. On it the little girl was laboriously lettering her ABC's with a chunk of soft red rock. Chris Beth's throat ached with compassion. What she couldn't do with a little of the money she had always taken for granted!

At recess time an eighth-grade boy (he claimed) sauntered up. "Miss Chrissy, this is my baby sister," he said.

Yes, she remembered the frail, frightened little girl.

"Ma wanted I should tell you she ain't had no time, so she ain't learnt her nothin'."

Chris Beth supposed the gawkish boy's explanation would have been amusing at one time. Even now, it would make a "cute little story" for some afternoon tea back home. But to her, these children's teacher, it was heartbreaking.

There's an awful gap between us, she thought. But somehow that was no threat anymore. *Neither they nor I can push through it. But I understand boys and girls. And they understand me. I'll do what everybody else does in this new land. I'll simply build a stile across that gap and we'll all climb over!*

And there was an "awful glory" in the thought, or was it a revelation?

18

Holy Joe

Even with the few books she had brought along, Chris knew there were not enough to go around. And none of them were alike. She wondered aloud just how to manage. These pioneer children, she had seen right away, were good decision-makers.

"I bet everybody's got one of these," one of the older boys suggested. He raised a rumpled sheet of fine-print paper—too fine to see from where Chris Beth stood at the front of the classroom.

A ripple of excitement told her that what the boy said was true. All but the beginners (who would be in a "chart class") pulled out a similar sheet of paper.

A single sheet! They were supposed to learn from that? And what on earth could it be, anyway?

"Can I read?" the boy asked eagerly.

Before she could say, *"May* I read?" the others had chimed in, each begging to read.

Chris Beth resisted the temptation to rap sharply on the box she called a desk. After all, she certainly did not want to dampen any enthusiasm that these students had for reading.

"I asked her first!" the older boy told the others.

"So he did," Chris Beth agreed. "You'll all get a turn, I promise. And then I'll read you a story."

As the boy stood, she checked the register to find his name.

Beltran. Beltran? Oh, yes, he was one of the "Basque" children that Nate had introduced. Sheep-raisers, weren't they? She checked the name again.

"Go ahead, Burton."

Burton, pleased that Miss Chrissy had remembered his name, grinned and said, "Mine's page 500." Then, haltingly, he began to read as Chris Beth digested the news that no pages matched.

"The…Lord…is…my…*shepherd!*" The last word came out triumphantly. Then the strange, surprising singsong continued, "I… shall…. not…*want!*"

Later Chris Beth realized that she had allowed Burton to read too long. The other children were moving restlessly. But she had been so torn between pity for the children who wanted so desperately to learn and shock that they had nothing to read but a page from the Bible (though they liked reading it) that time meant nothing to her. Was this where they had left off last year?

Still trying to work her way through the maze of emotions, Chris Beth allowed the children to read one by one. But she did remember to call time so that each would get a turn. When the last reader finished, she announced that they would take an early recess.

But the children were having no part of it. "Story story!" they all cried. "You promised!"

Well, so she had. Chris Beth reached for a copy of *Grimm's Fairy Tales*.

But again the children changed her plans. "Wait till we're ready to go home for that one! We want to hear 'Noah Zark'…No, 'Daniel and the Lion's Den'…Ump-uh, 'David 'n Goldilocks'!"

It was impossible for Chris Beth to keep a straight face at the titles. Taking her smile as consent, they leaned forward on the rough-board tables. "She's gonna!" whispered the "Baby Sister" Ma hadn't "learnt." There was pin-drop quiet.

Chris Beth fumbled through her literature books. Somewhere there were some Bible stories in one of them, she remembered. She had fallen into this trap somehow, but what was the harm, she supposed, just this once? Finally she came upon the story of the baby Moses' rescue by Pharoah's daughter.

"But before I read," she said to the waiting children, "will one of you tell me where the pages you're reading came from?"

"The Holy Bible!"

Well, she had asked for that one!

"I mean," she rephrased, "how did you each come to have a page?"

"Teacher let us use 'em," the older Smith boy defended. "A Holy Joe come by givin' 'em away, page at a time."

The rest of the children nodded.

A Holy Joe?

Their name for a preacher, young Wil told her. And the way he said *their* name set himself quite apart.

"Thank you for telling me," Chris Beth said quietly. "But we will not be using that title for a preacher—or anybody else. It's improper and it's—" she struggled for a word, "wrong," she concluded.

As she read the story, Chris Beth noted that every eye was upon her. Did they enjoy stories this much, or was there something about this particular one? Or was it the Bible in general? Nobody had prepared her for this. Nobody had prepared her for the children's begging—*pleading*—with her to read another and another.

"It's past recess time—"

"We don't care!" they cried in unison.

Chris Beth closed the book. "But I've run out of stories."

"Then read this," and before she could stop him, Burton Beltran was handing her the Twenty-Third Psalm.

Never had children touched her so much. The lump in her chest moved up into her throat, threatening to bring uncontrolled tears. In that emotional state, she began:

"The Lord is my shepherd; I shall not want." As she read, the memory came back that she used to read this passage over and over. She knew *how* it should read, to her surprise. The words flowed softly and sweetly—she knew this was so—until she finished: "And I will dwell in the house of the Lord *forever!*"

To her surprise, she had emphasized the final word as had Burton when he read. *Why?* She wondered as she dismissed the children with a wave of her hand.

As Chris Beth reached beneath her desk for the balls to be distributed to the children, she was aware suddenly of a shadow in the doorway. And there stood Joe.

"I've come to ask for your help," he said quietly. "I—I heard you read and—I—could I be one of your students?"

"You mean—here—I don't understand."

I'm fumbling for words as much as he is, she thought.

"Anywhere. The place doesn't matter." He had regained his composure and seemed to try to put her at ease.

"But why—on what? I mean in what area do you need help?"

"Reading," he smiled. "You see, I'm studying to be what you might call a Holy Joe."

19

Born-Again Teacher!

A week passed. Chris Beth hurried to school an hour before the children in an effort to be well-prepared for the trying day ahead. She stayed until darkness spread over the valley. She overheard Mrs. Malone express concern to O'Higgin, who had taken to practically living at Turn-Around Inn since the weather had grown damp. "Colder'n north side of an igloo, it is, down 'longside the branch." It was a surprise to learn that his quarters were only a tent to sleep in. It must be miserable.

"Should build a cabin like normal folks," Mrs. Malone sniffed when he complained.

"Should live me in a house."

"House!" she said sharply, then reddened when the Irishman grinned in agreement.

Both women knew that O'Higgin's services were nearly indispensable. Ned could never carry on alone with the milking, caring for the cattle and stock, cultivating, and harvesting—not to mention constant sawing down trees and blasting out stumps in the preparation of new cultivating ground.

But O'Higgin's presence about the place offered more than two helpful hands. There was a real need for a man in the household—with the children, yes, but Chris Beth suspected that Mrs. Malone secretly welcomed his male companionship in spite of her constant claims of "bein' no leaner." They discussed everything, including Chris Beth herself.

"She's workin' past time for the cows to come home, and it can be downright dangerous."

"I'll speak with the lassie," and for once O'Higgin was serious.

Chris Beth knew they were right. She was working hard. Once she would have felt driven to succeed, and for the wrong reasons. There would have been a need to save face, both with friends and family back home and *herself*. But now the reasons were different. There was born within her a new commitment, a burning desire to help these children learn in whatever way they learned best. If they liked to hear her sing, she would sing! And if they liked to read from the Bible, they would do that, too! Under different circumstances she could have laughed at herself, the "born-again" teacher.

Somewhere in back of her busy mind, Chris Beth knew that there were problems to be resolved, some of them pressing, but they would have to wait their turn. The brooch…a place to live…Vangie's future…a letter to Mama as to why her half-sister's coming West was out of the question…some alternate plan that Mama would never be able to come up with in her own helplessness.

And then suddenly would come the realization that the problems were simply on a treadmill, going nowhere toward solution. She was just too busy, too tired.

Then something else would try to push itself from below the surface of her subconscious mind. Joe—Joseph Craig—*a preacher?* Why should she be concerned? She shouldn't be, but she was. *Angry?* No—not now. *Glad?* She didn't know.

"All right," she would say aloud at those times. "So I do have problems. So do these children!"

And the new Chris Beth would reenter her private world of cutting out letters of the alphabet, preparing sums to write on the battered blackboard, and underlining passages she wished to read from the New Testament. Maybe a discussion would be helpful after reading? She had chewed her cedar pencil in concentration on that one. Of course it would be helpful! And maybe some chart stories, too, for the beginners. The older children could do the artwork.

Chris Beth was unaware that as she worked her face had taken on a new glow. But Mrs. Malone noticed—not that she could mention it to anybody. There was only O'Higgin to talk to. And that silly gander was wearing the same shine! The difference was that she didn't know Chris Beth's secret.

20

Lesson in Waiting

Chris Beth was wearing her new glow, enhanced by the rose wool shawl Mrs. Malone had knitted for the chilly evenings, when Joe came for his first lesson. Lesson in what she wasn't exactly sure; she only knew that he had mentioned help in reading.

"You look lovely," he told her as she took his hat at the door of Turn-Around Inn.

Now why should that simple compliment embarrass her? Chris Beth knew that color stained her face and hated herself for the schoolgirl silliness. *When young men paid me compliments back home, I thanked them. When Wilson North says the same words, I'm offended. And what's the matter with me anyway that I keep comparing these two men!* Then, for the first time, came the awareness that Jonathan Blake had not entered her mind at all.

The realization was so startling that her words were more abrupt than she intended in the curt "Thank you" to Joe. Then softening, she asked, "How may I be of help, Joe?"

"Wh—what was your reaction to my being a—a preacher?"

"I'll answer your question with one of my own: 'What has my reaction to do with it?'"

"A lot—everything."

We're talking around the subject, not about it, Chris Beth knew. The fact was that they were talking about their feelings without bringing them out in the open. That was unlike her—probably unlike Joe, too—but was there really anything to discuss?

Joe broke the silence. "Would you rather have known sooner?"

Chris Beth shook her head. "I couldn't have accepted it sooner," she said truthfully.

"Then I was right in waiting?" He reached for her hand. Chris drew back, and to her surprise, Joe laughed. "And I'm prepared to wait some more."

"The reading—" she began faintly and was surprised to find her heart was running away foolishly.

Later, reviewing the events of the evening, Chris Beth felt a deep admiration for Joe's acceptance of her little rebuff and his willingness to delve into the business at hand unself-consciously. The fact was, she admired everything about this quiet man. But there were to be no romantic involvements.

"It's the stuttering. I'm going to need this voice in a pulpit, heaven knows—no irreverence! I only stammer badly when I'm embarrassed or when I read—" He paused.

"We'll work on it," she promised

And without further ado, the lessons began. So did Joe's waiting, she knew.

21

A Clash of "Wils"

Chris Beth turned from the chalkboard where she was writing "Articulation Words" from *McGuffey's Fourth Reader* that she had brought from the school in the South. The children had come so far so fast, she thought with pride. It was good that she herself had taken all those speech-improvement courses in Boston, where they teased her about her slurred vowels. This way she could pronounce distinctly and have the children repeat after her.

Of course, young Wil had been a help. He was an excellent student, had a grasp on the reading skills, and was willing to help others. But he was a bit of a problem, too. There were times when he daydreamed—looking wistfully out the window when he should have been doing his sums. Generally he chose arithmetic time to go into his little dream world, and, if coaxed out of it, spent his time pulling Sadie Goldsmith's braids or tickling the bottom of anybody seated in front of him with a feather poked through the crack of a log-seat. And he knew every crack!

In spite of his mischief-making, Chris Beth thought as she looked at the entire student body, *I love every hair on each head, but there's something so special about this one.* Yes, no doubt about it, he was her favorite if she allowed herself to have one. But she refused to let it show. And something about this little sprite let her know that he wouldn't appreciate being "teacher's pet."

"Wil," she spoke from the front of the class. "Will you come up and recite now?"

Chris Beth listened to his reading and checked his arithmetic paper. Finding it less than half-finished, she asked him why. "I don't like it—didn't like it in Portland either! Teacher was a grouch."

Portland? She ignored the *grouch*.

Went to school there till end of school last year. Visited this summer.

Did he like it here?

Shrug.

What part did he like best?

Baseball. Until she took his ball.

The conversation had been quiet, and the nine-year-old had been polite. Still, Chris Beth felt that she had failed to communicate the importance of mastering addition and subtraction. Here was a fine mind that she was not going to see wasted.

She checked the register to find the name of his parents. Several names were still missing, and Wil's parents were among them.

Their little talk had apparently done no good. Wil sat gazing out the window instead of completing the arithmetic paper. Chris Beth went back and whispered that he should finish, as literature time was coming in a few minutes. He enjoyed that, she knew. The boy nodded, took up his pencil, and began what appeared to be the picture of a musket, the best she could tell from the corner of her eye. Well, it had to stop. A note at the end of the week. Today, if this kept up.

The climax came in literature class. "How many memorized a part of 'Hiawatha'?" she asked, and was pleased to see several hands go up. She had read them the poem yesterday, explained its meaning, and assigned as extra credit any favorite lines they wished to commit to memory.

"Volunteers?" she asked.

Most of the children were shy, looking at each other instead of her. Not Wil! As usual, he called out, "Let me be first, Miss Chrissy."

Maybe the recognition would do him good. "Fine, Wil."

Young Wil stepped forward. His face had the look of an angel, but there was a gleam in his eye that she had come to recognize.

Loudly and clearly—and, yes, beautifully, she had to admit—he recited, then stopped as if to make sure he had the attention of the entire class. Or did he need prompting? She glanced at her book. "…And the *naked* old Nakomis…" as the others burst into smothered giggles, then uncontrolled laughter.

There was no need in going on with the class. Wisely, Chris Beth announced recess 15 minutes early.

"Wil!" she called above the din of voices. "Remain in a minute, please."

When he was beside her, Chris Beth said, "I tried to talk earlier and we didn't get as far as I had hoped. Then you upset the class."

"I know," he surprised her by saying.

"I think we should have a little talk with your parents, and I'd like to have you sit in on it."

Wil sat silent.

"Would you like that?"

He shook his head but said nothing.

"I'm going to invite your mother—"

"She's not here!" The words were spoken fiercely.

"Then I will write to your father. He would be your legal guardian."

"But he—I can't—I don't want—" Tears were about to overflow.

"Please don't argue," she said firmly. "It's for your own good."

She wrote a little "To whom it may concern" note, explaining that she would like to have the guardian of Wil Ames come for a conference Monday after school.

Young Wil looked at her reproachfully for a moment, then squared his young shoulders and shot her the roguish smile she had come to associate with trouble. "A clash of wills," he grinned.

22

When Tongues Are Loosed

On Sunday the settlers gathered at Turn-Around Inn as planned. The circuit-riding Jonas Brown was "pourin' out the glory" elsewhere, Mr. Goldsmith told the worshipers, but he was with them "in spirit." Chris Beth wondered what good he could do either group in that disembodied state and carefully avoided Wilson's eyes lest they smile at the quaint phrase.

She looked at the congregation instead. Their number surprised her. The front room was large indeed, but it was totally inadequate for the men, women, and children who had flocked there on this dreary November day. It was probably an illusion, but the very walls of the sturdy house seemed to be bowed out as if it were letting its ribs expand in an effort to accommodate the usual group and the obvious newcomers.

After the singing, O'Higgin laid down his tuning fork and "opened the doors of the church" in an invitation to all who "felt the spirit increased inside" to give testimonials. Chris Beth watched and listened intently as one by one the men rose to speak of the blessings in their everyday lives. "Apples for all who come a'callin'…grain for the motley cattle…'nuf eggs to oversupply the general store…and all the love You drop from the windows of heaven." One or two read haltingly (less well than their children) from "the Good Book," and some only held the Bible up in silent reverence. *They are unable to read at all,* she thought. The realization touched her heart. *All the more reason I must redouble my efforts, not slow down.*

Suddenly a familiar voice broke into her reverie. Joseph Craig was reading, "The Lord is my shepherd; I shall not want."

The words of the beautiful psalm were familiar to Chris Beth. What touched her so deeply was Joe's deep, throaty voice, his perfect articulation—and the drama of it all. Tears stung behind her eyelids. Her heart drummed heavily in her chest, and there was a throbbing in her throat. *I'm trembling like a leaf* she thought. Yet there was such an unexplainable joy within that she wanted to shout "Amen!" when he finished.

As all heads bowed for the benediction, Chris Beth allowed the tears to roll unashamedly down her face. Let Maggie look. Let the whole world see—see that she felt pride in this humble man and the private little miracle that someway, somehow, she had helped loose his tongue. And, yes, let them all see what she knew now—that some invisible hand had moved their callings closer together. The two of them had a job to do in this settlement. So let *all* tongues be loosed!

23

Boston Buck

Sunday's startling revelation brought with it a reminder that great visions are no more than that unless the one to whom they're given puts them to work. There was a need to be practical. The valley was destined to boom—Chris Beth felt that. As more settlers came, the school would need enlarging, and there would be need for a church. Money would be a real problem, so Mrs. Malone certainly needed space as she offered temporary quarters for worship services to the increasing congregation.

So, Chris Beth decided, *with every conference, beginning with Monday's, I'll inquire about lodging.* Maybe young Wil's father would know of somebody who would take in a temporary boarder. Then if Vangie did come—oh, dear, she must get a note to Mama.

She had written note after note saying that her half-sister, in that "delicate condition" (for Mama's sake she couldn't call it "pregnancy") just must not travel. Always at that point she would pause, wonder what to say next, and then discard the letter. Maybe she should write to Vangie instead—only Vangie wasn't living there. She had better talk to Mrs. Malone. No, she had her share of problems. Joe?

Waiting after school on Monday for Wil's father, Chris Beth pondered further what to do. At least it was good to be able to think clearly. Maybe answers would come.

Suddenly she was aware that a shadow had fallen across the door. Rising from behind her desk, she stepped forward. "Mr.—"

But the figure she saw was the half-nude body of the first Indian she had ever seen. Her first impulse was to cry out, but something about the eyes which pierced hers silenced her. As he stealthily moved closer, she saw strange markings on the muscular body, crude shapes painted with what looked to be berry juices. A beaded band held back the straight, black hair that fell below his shoulders.

And then he reached as if to touch her. She drew back in panic. What did a lone woman do to defend herself? There was no escape— no back door—and where was Wil's father?

He took another step forward, still reaching, but his hand closed around her paisley satchel before it reached her. With sucked-in breath, Chris Beth watched in terror as the man opened the bag and emptied its contents on the floor. In horror she saw that the pearl-and-sapphire brooch lay at the Indian's bare feet. With a grunt of satisfaction, he stooped, picked it up, and pinned it in his heavy hair. Then, wordlessly, he turned toward the door.

A movement at the window caused Chris Beth to look up. What appeared to be a whole tribe was trying to crawl into the classroom. In paralyzed awe, she waited.

What happened next startled Chris Beth as much as the Indians. There was a loud "Boom!" Fire seemed to fly in all directions and the room filled immediately with sulfurous black smoke. The Indians let out cries of fear and fled into the forest, except for the Indian who had taken the pin. He lay prostrate on the dirt floor, writhing and moaning. Surely he must be mortally wounded.

Before she could decide what to do, a familiar voice issued a command, "Give the lady her bag!"

Wilson—Wilson was here! But how? Why? And then she saw him put a warning finger to his lips. She waited, unsure for what.

The Indian rose, but stood in sullen silence, making no move in her direction.

"More fire?"

"No!" There was panic in the Indian's eyes. Still, he was unwilling to do as Wilson had commanded. "Boston name," he said.

Wilson appeared to be considering the exchange. "You win," he conceded. "You are brave, but sometimes unwise. If I give you a Boston name, will you leave the lady alone? She lives here now."

"Boston—Boston;" She could see that he agreed to the pact.

"From now on you shall bear proudly the name of Buck—Boston Buck! Now return the bag *and* the pin."

Boston Buck did as told and ran away happily chanting, "Name Boston Buck, name Boston Buck!"

And what happened next startled her even more. Chris Beth remembered later that the room grew fuzzy. She swayed on her feet and would have fallen except that Wilson's arms were around her.

Everything that had happened was an incredible dream. But the arms around her were very real—undeniably reassuring. It seemed very natural that he should be there as she broke into uncontrollable sobs.

Wilson smoothed the strands of hair that had eased from her prim hairdo, winding it around his fingers as he did so. "Go ahead, cry," he soothed as one would soothe a child.

"It's just that I get one thing resolved—or think I do—and then something worse happens—and I get in deeper, till I can't handle anything—" Chris Beth knew she was blubbering but she had no power to stop. "And you laugh at me."

"Not anymore." He was right, she realized, but she felt too weary to answer.

He continued softly, "Why must you go on fighting life so hard? Why can't you be like the rest of us and just lean a little?"

"I've been hurt that way." The fatigue was closing in.

"Mostly your pride, I'd say. And we've all been hurt, my dear."

For no good reason, she felt the tears again. Wilson brushed them away gently. "Let's not fight anymore. You're among friends—not in enemy territory. And there's so much we need to talk about."

He had spoken the truth, of course. She drew back. "You first," she said. And together they sat down on one of the split logs, with his arm still around her. And there, in the comforting circle, Chris Beth listened to Wilson North's story, less surprised by it than by her unquestioning acceptance.

What Will People Say?

The sun had shone briefly as she and Wilson talked, but as they left the schoolhouse, clouds gathered again. In the sudden downpour that followed, the two of them were drenched. Chris Beth had grown accustomed to the Oregon Country's sudden moods—its sun and rain, with rainbows between. She didn't mind. As they rode in the rain, visions of Mama and Vangie's rushing to close the shutters came to mind. In a storm, Mama would get a headache and little Vangie would wrap her head in the duck-down pillow.

I'm glad I told Wilson about Vangie's coming, but guarded the details, she thought. *When?* She didn't know. And, of course, Wilson had too much style to ask *why.* In fact, *why's* seemed of no importance to the wonderful people of the settlement.

It was growing dark and Wilson would ride with her to Turn-Around Inn, he told her. Having said so much already, there seemed to be no further need for words. Chris Beth was glad. It gave her an opportunity at least to review some of what Wilson had told her. Sorting it all out and putting it into some kind of perspective would take a long time. That made no difference. They had covered enough ground to make her heart sing like the meadowlark who seemingly was undaunted by neither rain nor approaching twilight.

It was good to know about the Indians. Most of them were on the reservation. "Boston Buck" had refused to go, preferring the ways of the "Bostons." He was given to wandering around—even in and out of houses on occasion—but he meant no harm, Wilson explained. Nuisance though he sometimes was, he more than made up for it by showing the settlers the best fishing waters, where the wild raspberries and strawberries grew, and how to trap game and dig clams. "The grasshoppers we can do without," Wilson had chuckled.

Chances were slim that the Indian would return, and, if he did, it would be as her friend. As to the others, they were strangers—probably wandered in from the reservation. They probably came out of curiosity. Still, Wilson had deemed it wise to use his usual "magic" just in case. The explosive concoction was a little trick he used when tramping around in a strange patch of woods looking for certain botanical species for his book. "They can't quite figure whether I'm a madman or a god! Just as well keep 'em guessing."

Indians disposed of, Chris Beth had asked how on earth Wilson just happened to be there when she needed him. He didn't "just happen" to be on hand, of course.

"You sent for me, remember?"

The only person she had sent for was Wil's father.

"Guardian," he corrected. "I'm the to-whom-it-may concern!"

As Chris Beth's overtaxed mind tried to absorb still another shock, Wilson explained. His sister had made an unfortunate marriage to an irreputable drummer who divided his time between liquor and dance-hall women. Eventually, he left her with a small child, a fact she had been unable to accept. Wilson had paused there, biting his lip to control his emotions, and Chris Beth guessed that a broken heart had caused the young mother to take her own life.

"My father was killed shortly afterward in an accident at the grist mill. It was more than my mother's weak heart could stand." The three of them were buried in a little family plot behind the big house where he and young Wil lived now. *How sad for them all.*

"But I have the boy," he said proudly. "I tried sending him away to school for his own good, summers too, but he got homesick. He's a bright youngster—isn't he?" He hesitated.

"Oh, very!" Chris Beth assured him. "Fact is, he's outsmarting me. We'll talk about his interests. I can help him better now that I know." Suddenly she laughed. "I understand now what our little wizard meant when he said there would be a 'clash of wills'!"

Wilson nodded. *"Wils,* he meant. My namesake." And again she noted the pride in Wilson's voice.

They had talked some more about Wil's study habits and agreed upon a program to follow. Then they had talked about Chris Beth's predicament.

"There are some things I don't feel like discussing," she said slowly.

"No need to." But somehow Chris Beth had the feeling that he knew some of them already.

"Joe and I have talked about a place for you to stay and come to the conclusion that there is a very simple solution. Promise to go along with it?"

"Oh, yes!" she cried impulsively. "Anything, *anything!"*

Immediately he was the old Wilson. "Lady, you got yourself a deal! I'm helping Joe move in with young Wil and me tomorrow. The big house's far more than we two need. So Joe's cabin is yours."

Chris Beth felt her eyes widen. *Try to act calm,* she told herself. Maybe she pulled it off, but inside her stomach churned.

"That would be—uh, unwise." I sound like Mama, she thought.

"Afraid of living just whistling distance from us?"

She stiffened. "Of course not! But what would people say?"

Wilson North hooted. "That's the old Christen Elizabeth, the Southern belle with the Boston accent, speaking."

"Let me think," she whispered, but deep inside she knew what the answer had to be.

25

Anticipation

In a warm flannel robe and with her hair loosed and drying by a crackling fire, Chris Beth shared the events of the day with her close friend. Mrs. Malone hung onto every word, nodding between mouthfuls of huckleberry cobbler and hot coffee. "Don't have your knack for rollin' out pastry," Mrs. Malone explained.

"It couldn't be better this way," Chris Beth said, savoring every bite after the strange, emotional day.

After seconds, there was a lull. Mrs. Malone then asked, "Did Wilson tell you he's studyin' to be a doctor?"

"Doctor?" Chris Beth was stunned.

"The same," the older woman said, picking up the dishes.

"But he's a botanist and is writing a book—besides the grist mill—"

"And studying' to be a doctor," Mrs. Malone repeated. "Some special big name—path-o-something, havin' to do with diseases."

"Pathology."

"Could be. Course, we hope he takes to doctorin'. Doc's getting past house-callin', you know, and Wilson'll be needed."

Very true. *How nice it would be for the settlement,* Chris Beth thought. And the vision returned. The valley would grow...there would be a teacher...a preacher...and now a doctor. And she was a part of the trio! Strange, she thought drowsily, how she would have been annoyed that Wilson failed to tell her this just a short while ago. But there were matters she hadn't revealed either. And it seemed to make no difference.

Chris Beth patted a yawn and tried to listen to Mrs. Malone. It seemed that she too had some news. "Guess what!" She sounded very excited. "The President is coming through—the President and his First Lady! They will stop over at the Pass, folks say, and the Presidential Coach itself will be turnin' right up here at our corner, Oh—" she dreamed, "if only we had Turn-Around Inn ready—who knows?"

"You will, someday," Chris said with conviction.

Mrs. Malone nodded and then went on excitedly. "O'Higgin has promised to take me to the turnoff. I've been studyin' the catalogue for latest fashions and all."

It was good to see her so excited. But there was more. "Folks say this is the coach that has the 'gallant white steeds' we read about and that the coach is trimmed in real gold. Don't you think you oughta see Nate and ask that the children meet the party?"

Well, of course! That was a wonderful idea. Then she gave way to languor and anticipation...

26

Going to Meet the President

On Monday of the "big week," young Wil asked Chris Beth if he could erase the chalkboard. The request was a peace offering, she knew, and she accepted it as a truce. "What's more, as soon as you've finished back assignments, I'll have you help Wong with language."

"Then, can—may I have my ball back?"

She nodded. "And work on your leaf collection."

It was always good to establish a warm student-teacher relationship, but this one was imperative. Chris Beth, with the aid of the Malone children, had moved her few possessions into Joseph Craig's cabin while Wilson helped him move to the North house. Young Wil's attitude could make or break the success of what in her mind was a questionable arrangement at best.

But she loved the cabin! The inside logs were hewed smooth, the cracks were chinked against the wind, and the floors, though fir, were polished to a hardwood shine. The fireplace was small but surrounded by bright, hand-braided rugs big enough, Chris Beth thought, to stretch out and dream upon when time allowed.

Joe left the furniture—rare walnut bureau, high-poster bed, and round oak dining room table and chairs—which, though beautiful, made the cabin look like a doll house. The heirloom pieces had belonged to his parents, Joe told her, as they worked to complete the moving. The Craigs and Norths had come West over the Applegate Trail and, though forced to abandon most of their Eastern furniture in the steep descent, had salvaged these few, making them doubly precious. Then, the awful fire! It had destroyed the big house up by the waterfall, leaving little but this furniture and the few dishes (which she was welcome to use).

Chris Beth saw that the fire was a painful subject so had decided not to pursue it, when Joe volunteered the reason for his pain. "I lost them both that night—my father and mother. We tried to fight our way through to Dad, but the roof caved. Mother lived only a few hours after we pulled her from the flames. I guess that's one reason Wil decided to go into medicine." He inhaled deeply. "I pray that there'll never be another forest fire here."

"I'm so sorry," Chris Beth had said, reaching for Joe's hand. His large, capable hand had closed over her small, taut fist momentarily. Then, gently he eased her fingers open and straightened them into a relaxed position. His touch was a near-caress.

The tragedies that these people of the settlement had lived through left Chris Beth humbled. Compared to their problems, her own looked as off-scale in size as the antique furniture in the little cabin. But that was not why she clung to Joe's warm hand longer than necessary. It felt so reassuring, so powerful, and so—something else for which she could find no name...

So, with the move made, the larder stocked with enough of Mrs. Malone's chili sauce, apple butter, and succotash to feed the cavalry, the bed piled high with quilts, and a load of backlogs hauled over by O'Higgin, Chris Beth had gone back to school with a singing heart. Not only was she settled (temporarily, at least), but she had a carrot to dangle in front of her young charges' noses. Who *wouldn't* work hard with the promise that maybe—just maybe—the school board would let them meet the stage and see the nation's President! That was, *if* the weather permitted, *if* parents would help with transportation, *if*—

But why go on? The children were so excited they would hear not another word! *And I'm no better,* she thought.

Friday dawned bright and clear. A light frost melted away with the sun's rays, but patches clung to sweetbrier vines that wound around the fence rows. It was a "mitten mornin' for shure," O'Higgin had declared, and Chris Beth cautioned all the children to button up snugly as they piled excitedly into the waiting wagons. She herself rode with Wilson, whose silly cart looked a little more respectable with the gaudy umbrella put away for the winter. Thoughtfully, he tucked a lap robe over her knees but paused before climbing in beside her. "Forgot something," he apologized.

"Oh, no! Not Esau." But Wilson was out of hearing distance.

To her relief, it was not the dog he brought back. It was the black bag, a telltale tool of his profession.

Briefly, Chris Beth wondered why the doctor's kit should make her apprehensive. That was silly. So thinking, she put it out of her mind, concentrating instead on the stark beauty of the woods.

27

The Unexpected!

How different this ride was from the first one through the forest! Chris Beth had difficulty identifying with the person she had been then. It was as if she had been given a new body before her time!

That reminded her of Wilson's bag in back of the hack. He wasn't a doctor yet, so why the kit?

He smiled at her question. "Well, the truth is that I *am* ready for practice, but I've been trying to decide exactly how much of my life I want to give over to research or general practice—" His voice trailed off. "As to the supplies, I always take them along. A doctor has to expect the unexpected, you know."

She supposed so, little realizing just how right he was. The sun was noon-high and Chris Beth was sure the children would be hungry. "Maybe we should stop at the next clearing for lunch."

Wilson nodded. "Plenty of time. Stage is due at two."

Lunch completed, the wagons moved on toward the fateful place, where the driver had announced "End of the trail!" in words that carried a doomsday ring. *Well, things were different now,* she thought happily, as she helped parents unload children for a romp before the arrival of the President of the United States! Joe, she remembered, would be "riding shotgun" on the stage again. Somehow that gave her a feeling of pride—similar to the feeling she had when she saw Wilson check his medical supplies before joining in the children's play. Someday she must analyze these feelings.

The rumble of the carriage wheels was audible long before the line of stagecoaches appeared. How many? Chris Beth gasped as she counted six gleaming coaches, one of them drawn by white horses— undoubtedly the President's! Her excitement grew as quiet spread over the children. Mrs. Malone's eyes, she saw, were as big as theirs.

As the party neared, she tried to make out the names newly painted on the outside of the vehicles: SHASTA EXPRESS, OVER-LAND, and CALIFORNIA STAGE. The latter must house the President, she was sure. It was a study in color, with wheels, tongue, and running gear painted bright canary-yellow and outlined with black stripes through which were spaced single red roses. The body was olive green with large hand-painted landscape scenes on the panels. Around the neck of each horse was a chain of ivory rings. The driver, not to be outdone, wore fine buckskin gloves, fancy-stitched jacket and pants, and silver-buckled boots. The finery tattled of the "back East" shops familiar to Chris Beth but foreign to the settlers. The pretentiousness of it all looked a little disgusting to her after her months here with open, unpretending people. Still, she welcomed the experience for the children and suspected that the adults were equally awed.

Mrs. Malone proved that. "Well, I never in my born days!" she exclaimed in appreciation of all the pomp.

"Have ye a look at the whiplash!" whispered O'Higgin.

"Big enough it be fer towin' another coach, it is!"

"Precisely," Wilson whispered back. "And strong enough to serve as a noose for a highwayman."

"Be ye sober" Wilson's grim nod said that he was.

As the caravan drew to a stop, all eyes focused on the Presidential Coach. But something drew Chris Beth's attention to the last vehicle, which creaked along in front of a heavily loaded supply wagon, drawn by mules and manned by rugged drivers. Sometimes they all traveled together like this for safety, she remembered hearing. This would be especially true with such a dignitary aboard. As cheers went up, she knew that the President must have made an appearance, but she continued to stare at a face she had seen through the window of the back coach. "Oh, it can't be—" she whispered. And, without realizing she had done so, she grabbed Wilson's arm for support. He followed her gaze to where a fragile girl was being helped from aboard the coach where Joe rode as "Shotgun Messenger."

"Vangie," she whispered. And, even as she spoke, she saw her lovely sister crumple to the ground.

28

Appalling Emotions

Whatever emotions she had expected of the reunion vanished at the sight of her sister. The shock of seeing her emerge from the stagecoach, the simultaneous fear that clutched her own heart as Vangie fainted, and the actual wonder of her being here in such an unexpected fashion were too much to absorb without recoil. Like a windup toy, whose action might stop at any moment, she rushed forward with Wilson to where the willow-thin girl lay on the ground. Thank heavens, the others had crowded around the Presidential party, giving the two of them room to get through.

A shaft of sun broke through the trees, highlighting Vangie's pale blond hair with shades of new copper. The beautiful blue eyes were closed, but Chris Beth noted with alarm that the deep circles around them were almost as deep a violet. And the tiny figure, always slender, was now wafer-thin. *She looks like a priceless Dresden doll,* she thought as always about her younger sister. And, as always, she wanted to gather Vangie in her arms and comfort her until her hurts went away. But there was no time. Wilson had scooped up the fragile figure with practiced skill and rushed to wrap her in the woolen lap robe. "Fainted," was all he said.

Wilson North had moved quickly, but not quickly enough for Chris Beth could see the raw emotions on his taut face. There she read a tenderness she had never seen before. She recognized the look. It went beyond professional concern and into the heart.

When Vangie's eyelids fluttered, Chris Beth would have moved forward, but a Wilson she had never seen before restrained her. "Go back with the Malones!" he ordered. "I'm taking her with me!"

Mechanically, she stepped back, waiting for the hurt to come. "Chris—Chrissy—" Vangie tried to whisper. "I'm sorry—"

"Don't talk," Wilson whispered softly. "I'll take care of you." He dismissed Chris Beth with a jerk of his head and drove back toward his homestead. Why shouldn't *she* be with Vangie?

Joe spoke from behind her, and she turned in surprise and near-annoyance to see him leaning against a giant fir. She wondered if he had witnessed her humiliation at being pushed aside—even though, the reasonable side of her said for good cause. But when he spoke, his voice was normal. "Harmony and Amelia are riding back with friends. Miss Mollie has room for you and me."

O'Higgin helped her into the spring seat that she and Joe would occupy before climbing up beside Mrs. Malone in the driver's seat. Chris Beth wished that she and Joe—or she alone—could have ridden in back. *I'd like to dangle my feet and think.*

Instead, there was to be less privacy than she had imagined. Little Jimmy John, exhausted from the long day, fussed, refused his milk and tea cakes, and insisted on riding with Chris Beth.

"Child misses you powerful like," Mrs. Malone said. "I don't get time to read the Bible stories like you did. Funny thing—this one takes to the Old Testament tales. Remember the picture you showed 'im of the Promised Land and that big bunch o' grapes?"

Chris Beth remembered. It was from a favorite picture book of her childhood. The cluster of grapes, she remembered, was so enormous that two men had to run a stick through the fruits and share the load. What she couldn't recall was where the book came from. Someone had shared it with her. But who?

Jimmy John was squirming sleepily in her lap in need of attention. Not that she minded the interruption. She had tried to recall that missing chapter before, but always at this point her memory dissolved. The baby yawned, stuck a fat fist into his mouth, and fell asleep immediately. She pressed her lips against the soft hair on top of his head. She had missed him too, she realized.

Chris Beth was only aware that the others talked. Most of their conversation was lost. Try as she would, it was impossible to concentrate. Too much had happened. There were too many questions.

Most of the talk was about the "greatest thing that ever happened hereabouts," and Chris Beth realized with a start that she hadn't even seen the celebrated First Couple! Better listen, as she would need to be informed for classroom discussions. But she had lost interest in President Rutherford B. Hayes and his First Lady.

Joe had remained quiet. Chris Beth was surprised when he spoke quietly to her. "Glad I could be with Vangie while she waited."

Waited?

No room on stages for three days. Vangie had had to lay over in Redding, and hadn't seemed well. "She's exquisite," he added.

Chris Beth nodded yes to both his statements. Vangie was far from "well"—and apparently Wilson thought her "exquisite" too!

Then, realizing that she had not thanked him, she laid a hand on his sleeve. "Joe, I appreciate you."

"You'd better!" He grinned. And somehow she felt comfortable again. *Strange,* she thought, *how he always makes me feel this way.*

Typically, Joe fell silent as they rode farther into the woods. It was good to be allowed to think, or try to. It had been a strange, mixed-up day—a day that brought appalling emotions, some of which she had thought dead. When better than here with Joe to sort them out?

Naturally, it would be a surprise to see Vangie. And just as naturally her arrival brought its own set of problems, compounded by her obvious fragility. Chris Beth once again felt fury at her stepfather's treatment of his daughter, disappointment at her mother's helplessness, and resentment of the new burden when she was just making her own adjustment. *And I thought I'd put those feelings behind me,* she thought in confusion. Instead, another baffling emotion had sprung up to join them.

Yes, Chris Beth had to admit, Vangie's presence here had brought another kind of unhappiness. Maybe it was injured pride. Where there's no love, there could be no jealousy—could there? And she certainly was not in love with Wilson North—was she? Or was she as fickle as she had always thought Mama and Vangie to be? It was a disturbing thought—one she would do away with in short order. She was the strong one. No, it most certainly was not jealousy.

She had no love to give. But pride—that was another matter…

So engrossed was Chris Beth in her thoughts that she hardly realized that the winter's early darkness had closed in and they were in front of Turn-Around Inn.

Wolf barked happily. The children raced into the house and Chris Beth surrendered little Jimmy John to O'Higgin with a sigh of relief. She hadn't realized how heavy a two-year-old could be. Her arms were stiff and unfeeling as Joe helped her down from the seat of the wagon.

"You'll never know how right you looked holding the baby," he said.

"You'll never know how right I felt," she answered, regretting it immediately. What a ridiculous thing for an unmarried lady to say to a man! Particularly one who, as Mrs. Malone would have said, had "no prospects"! How very embarrassing.

To her added embarrassment, she felt Joe's eyes on her. It was a welcome help when Mrs. Malone called, "Now inside, *everybody!*"

"I have to check on Vangie—"

"Not on an empty stomach! She's with Wilson."

Yes, how well she knew.

29

A Tearful Forgiveness

Chris Beth lingered, looking inside the window as Joe hitched Dobbin outside the North home. He had insisted on going for his buggy while she helped Mrs. Malone with dishes.

"She may need me," was all he said to O'Higgin's offered ride.

Through the window, Chris Beth saw a scene which both warmed and frightened her. Firelight cast shadows about the large living room and reflected on the mellow beams above. Vangie sat bundled beside the hearth while Wilson peeled apples. She had put aside any feeling of jealousy—if that's what her initial emotion was—but her sister must not fall into another trap. And, she thought in strange contradiction, neither must Wilson. And, then, with a sudden surge of overpowering emotion, Vangie's presence here became a reality too good to be true no matter what the circumstances.

She rushed into the room, and Vangie, tripping over the blanket, rushed into her arms with a little moan. "Oh, Chrissy, Chrissy, don't ever leave me again—ever—ever—"

"Sh-h-h-h," Chris Beth smoothed damp curls from the feverish brow. Vangie, little Vangie, was again her baby sister, to be loved and protected against the world's evils. "I never will!"

The two men tiptoed unnoticed into the great kitchen.

For a long time both of them were silent, and then they both began talking at once, just as they always had. "One at a time," Chris Beth advised, "but slowly. Don't tire yourself now."

"Oh, Chrissy, it was awful, awful, his sending me away—calling me, a 'woman of the night' and saying God would punish the *baby*—" That would mean the pious "Father Stein"!

"I can imagine," Chris Beth said bitterly. "Try not to think about it. You're here now—with me—with us. You're safe!" And, as she spoke, she knew that it was true

"But," Vangie drew back uncertainly. Chris Beth was surprised to see fear in the younger girl's face. "How can you welcome me?"

"Why shouldn't I?"

"Didn't Mama tell you—I mean—?" Her voice trailed off faintly.

"About the baby? Of course." There was no need to tell Vangie that she had been so astonished and frightened herself at the time that she had burned the letter without reading it all.

Vangie was so still that Chris Beth wondered if she was all right. And then she spoke. "And you can forgive me? Knowing who fathered the child?" Her words were spoken in whispers.

But she *didn't* know, she was about to say. And then the cold, iron hand of fear gripped her heart. It wasn't true. It *couldn't* be! Vangie's blue eyes were looking at her piteously and she was cringing as she used to cringe at the feet of her father. "She *didn't* tell you." A sob caught in her throat. "It was," she whispered, "Jonathan Blake."

Although the words stung like an adder, later Chris Beth knew even then that hearing them spoken was more shocking than the impact of Vangie's confession. Somewhere, in a dream or in some far corner of her wounded heart, she had suspected—maybe even known. Vangie in Boston…her letters home saying she had seen Jonathan…his sudden cooling ardor. And always Vangie had wanted whatever Chris Beth possessed—first her strength, later her clothes, and finally her suitors—a woman in a child's body. *Odd*, she thought numbly, *I always thought of Mama exactly the opposite.*

"Don't hate me, Chrissy. Please—"

"I don't hate you, Vangie," Chris Beth said slowly and was surprised to know it was true. "It's all a tragic mistake, but not altogether your fault."

Vangie stiffened in her arms. "Oh, but it was! I envied you."

Chris Beth waited until the rigid body relaxed before answering. "I know," she said. "But you were a child, only 16."

"I'm 17 now!" Chris Beth almost smiled at her sister's defensiveness when she was so totally defenseless. But there was no trace of a smile in her heart. Vangie's mention of age reminded her that, although there wasn't that much difference in their ages, it was Chris Beth who must make some provision for the future. She hated herself for the vital question she had to ask.

"Vangie?" She inhaled deeply. "Vangie, did he offer to marry you?"

The girl's eyes, almost purple in the firelight, widened in shock, then closed in despair. "He's dead," she whispered. "Killed in a hunting accident."

Chris felt her own eyes dilate in shock. Jonathan alive was one thing. Jonathan dead was another. "One can't go on hating a dead person," she said more to herself than to Vangie.

Vangie's grip tightened around her. "Forgive me—" she begged again. And her sobbing told Chris Beth that Vangie had not forgiven herself.

"Vangie—" Whatever she was about to say was lost forever because at that point, she burst into tears herself.

It seemed like hours later that Vangie whispered, "I've cried myself dry," the words of their childhood.

Chris Beth responded in like manner. "So it's time to pray."

She was forever the "older sister," and it was up to her to take the lead. But how to begin? She was out of practice. But, as she remembered, the God of her childhood didn't demand eloquent prayers.

"Hello, Lord," she whispered. "It's been a long time…"

30

Secrets Revealed

It seemed to Chris Beth that she was sending up more than her fair share of prayers in the days that followed her sister's arrival in the settlement. But she guessed not, since the Lord was taking time to answer them all! Oh, it was good to be back—she smiled at the word—admittedly *leaning!* Everything was going to "right up," just as Mrs. Malone had promised. She could hardly wait until Thanksgiving to tell her friend about her countless blessings. She, Vangie, Wilson, and Joe had been so busy with "living," that, as Joe put it, it left no time for "visiting."

Of course, what the four of them shared was hardly visiting. She struggled for hours for a more fitting word. It was more like—well, she was back to that word again, *living*. And what on earth would the valley folk think she meant by that! She hardly knew herself what to make of the new relationship, let alone explain it to another. She had better do some thinking before they joined the crowd that Mrs. Malone and O'Higgin had invited to Turn-Around Inn for a holiday feast. She and Vangie *had* to move into the cabin. But details?

Well, there would be some details she would keep to herself. They belonged to her and Vangie. That wasn't quite true either, she was forced to admit. To her surprise, the two men of the new foursome knew the details she had hoped to keep secret. Even now, she wasn't sure, after the initial shock, if she was angry, embarrassed, or pleased. At least she was relieved to know that anything the four of them shared would go no further. *There would have been no way to hold some of it back anyway.*

Chris Beth pushed away from her desk and laid aside the papers she was grading to glance about the classroom. The children had filled the four corners with piles of cornstalks and fat pumpkins. The cornucopia (a real goat's horn, brought in by Nate Goldsmith, instead of the wicker one she had back home!) overflowed with pine cones, mellow fruit, and golden ears of grain. Truly, there was "abundant life" here—just another of the many things she would be praising the Creator for again come the day after tomorrow. Scoring the papers could wait. The boys and girls were doing so very well, some of them excelling, and over the four-day recess the men of the settlement were planning to floor the building. Oh! How wonderful! But for now she needed to think.

Thinking time was hard to find either at the cabin or at the big North house. Not that she minded. Maybe that was the problem. She didn't mind at all! Where was it all leading? How could she stop it? *Or,* she bit her lip in concentration, *did she want to?*

She supposed that it was she who, unwittingly, laid the foundation for the friendships which might be going beyond the usual definition of the word. Both men had befriended her in a grave time of need. And, though they were different from each other, she was attracted to them both. The perplexing part of it was that her feelings toward Joe and Wilson were as different as the two men were from each other. How could a woman possibly be thinking like this when she wasn't a candidate for love anyway!

With a burning face, Chris Beth returned to her work. The papers suddenly seemed important after all. The trouble was that she was unable to concentrate. Scraps of conversations kept coming back.

"Wilson figures the baby will be here toward the end of April," Vangie had said as matter-of-factly as if noticing the arrival of spring.

"He *knows?*"

"You mean the exact date? Of course he knows there's going to be a baby!" Something of the old lighthearted Vangie came back. "He knew the first day."

But of course he would have! Chris Beth felt foolish.

"Does he know—?" She let the question hang, hardly knowing how to phrase it.

"Who the father is?" Vangie shook her head. "It doesn't matter. But he knows that I'm not married, yes."

Another time when the two of them had talked, Chris Beth asked what *she* should tell people. *I sound like Mama,* she thought, and was disturbed at the likeness. Still, she did have to know what course of action to follow. The situation wasn't exactly ideal!

Vangie had laughed. "They'll *know* before too long!" she promised. Then, sobering, she added, "About the name, I'll just use my own. I guess it's good we're half-sisters, though I often wish we had had the same father."

Chris Beth had wished the same many times. But now was not one of them! The different surnames did offer a measure of protection for the unborn child. Then she began to realize that the baby's arrival would extend their family. Why, she would be an aunt! At one time the thought would have been unsavory, but now it was more than bearable. It was as sweet as honeycomb! She wondered what color eyes the baby would have—and hair. Would it be a boy or a girl? Waiting must be hard for Vangie. She could hardly wait herself.

Chris Beth again laid down her pencil. She was remembering something else. It was even more disturbing because it involved a secret all her own.

"Does Wilson intend telling Joe—I mean, the details?"

Vangie looked surprised and, in her usual candid—naive, really—manner, responded, "Oh, I told him myself when we had to wait in Redding."

"Vangie, you didn't—"

"Tell him about you? He knew already—except that it was the same man." The first part should have come as no surprise. She had been feverish on the stagecoach and he had been kind. But Jon's betrayal! Oh, the shame.

Chris Beth's reflections were interrupted by a faint rustling in the hazelnut bushes. Almost simultaneously, the door opened soundlessly. Boston Buck stepped inside.

Several times Chris Beth had thought she caught sight of the young Indian's head bobbing in and out of the thickets surrounding the school building. Hoping it was her imagination, she had tried to dismiss any worry that his presence might have caused.

Automatically her eyes went to her bag. The brooch was still there. Each day she had planned to wrap it here in privacy, and now (even as she faced possible danger, a part of her was thinking ahead) there would be nobody to whom she could return it.

The Indian approached cautiously. Then, as she wondered what to do, he pulled from behind him an enormous, beautifully feathered wild turkey!

Such a flood of surprise and relief flowed over her that for a moment Chris Beth was sure she would burst into tears. But that was the last thing she wanted to do. The gift deserved some dignity.

"Thank you, Boston Buck," she said bowing humbly. Then, taking a shimmering feather from the tail of the bird, she tucked it into her hair.

Whoever said Indians never smiled certainly had never met this one! A smile creased the dark face, revealing a set of perfect teeth. He moved forward, took a brilliant feather from the turkey's tail, and stuck it in his headband.

"Name Boston Buck," he said.

And then he was gone.

31

Surprise Marriage

The two men left before daylight on Thanksgiving morning in order to get the turkey into Mrs. Malone's oven before her hams. They would take Wilson's cart, they told Chris Beth and Vangie, leaving the buggy and Dobbin, the more dependable horse, for them. Young Wil went with the men, and the girls were to bring Esau. It was silly to take the dog, Chris Beth argued. But she was voted down.

Dogs are thankful too! That was Wilson.

Then let them have their "dog days"!

A measure of protection. That was Joe.

But they weren't afraid—

Who isn't? And besides, he's a dear. Vangie.

Chris Beth gave in grudgingly, but inside she was amused. It was always like this, with their good-natured (and sometimes heated) dialogue, after many a detour, ending up on "easy street." But in this instance, Vangie, though speaking lightly, seemed concerned about something.

"It's the dress—and young Wil," she admitted to Chris Beth. "I mean, I'll be among strangers, and I'm supposed to be widowed. What would be right, Chrissy?"

Yes, that did present a problem. Bright colors would be inappropriate. Chris Beth had misgivings about the implied deception. But there was the baby to think about.

They decided on a simple dark cotton dress with white linen collar and cuffs that made Vangie look like a little-girl Pilgrim wearing her mother's clothes. But, "I look tacky," she said.

Would it make her happier if Chris Beth wore her black skirt and pleated-bosom blouse? It would.

"But what about young Wil?" she asked Vangie.

The younger girl stopped brushing her hair. "He doesn't like me." And that seemed important.

"Young Wil's an introspective child," Chris Beth told her. "He's had more than his share of hurts, and it takes awhile for him to trust others."

"He likes *you*."

"I'm his teacher, Vangie, often the object of a child's first love. Give him time."

It was midmorning when the two of them reached Turn-Around Inn. The men stood around an outside fire where a whole pig was roasting. Smoke billowed from every chimney of the big house, and it was easy to imagine the happy bustle of aproned ladies inside. Mrs. Malone would be issuing orders faster than O'Higgin could carry them out and greeting guests at the same time.

But surprisingly to all, neither of them was in sight. They were greeted only by Wolf at the gate and Ambrose at the door.

Chris Beth noted with pleasure that the settlers gathered to greet the two of them immediately, as she had promised Vangie they would. Undoubtedly Maggie had spread the news, but the girl herself made no move toward them. The others welcomed Vangie warmly, so she wore a flush of happiness by the time Wilson elbowed his way to her.

"Where are our hosts?" Chris Beth asked Joe, who was close behind Wilson.

"Everybody's wondering," he replied, as he took her basket of food. She had worked late the night before preparing Boston baked beans and Southern spoon bread. "Might as well put a bit of all the cultures together," she had conspired with Vangie, who watched with more than her usual interest in cooking.

Chris Beth looked about the front room with appreciation as she hung her and Vangie's hooded capes in the closet. The Malone children had swung festoons of evergreen mingled with bright sprigs of bittersweet and sweet-smelling rose hips from the sweetbriers. She wondered what they would wash dishes in for the big crowd when every granite pot and pan available was filled with the last of the purple-and-bronze chrysanthemums. Was Thanksgiving always so festive? And so mysterious? An air of expectancy seemed to hang in the air to mingle with the smell of rising yeast bread and pumpkin pies.

Chris Beth felt the sense of security she had felt when this wonderful family had taken her in. The children gathered around her eagerly, all talking at once. Little Jimmy John tugged at her skirt until she scooped him up in her arms.

The day was all she had promised Vangie it would be, with two exceptions. The large crowd, exciting as it was, would probably make it impossible to get in a private word with Mrs. Malone. The other exception was a certain glint she read in Maggie Solomon's green eyes whenever they met her own. Each time the girl spoke with another of the guests, open hand to her mouth as if to guard some secret, her gaze returned to where Chris Beth, Vangie, Wilson, and Joe were visiting with neighbors. It was plain to see that she was discussing the four of them—and unfavorably.

"I'd better offer a hand in the kitchen," Chris Beth told Vangie. Probably best to break up the foursome for Maggie's benefit.

'Wilson answered for her sister. "I want Vangie to meet someone anyway. Young Mrs. Martin's here and expecting her first. She and you," he turned to Vangie, "will want to talk."

Chris Beth nodded. The Martins were the "new but learnin'" couple that Nate had introduced to her that Sunday at the brush arbor.

By the time Chris Beth was able to push through the crowd, a loud ring of the dinner bell outside drew everybody's attention.

"Brother Jonas," someone said. "Seems he's about to make an announcement."

The circuit rider stepped inside the back door, followed by men and children from out-of-doors. With a great deal of pomp, he brushed an imaginary bit of lint from his frock coat, stepped onto a rawhide-bottomed chair, cleared his throat importantly, and sang out: "Ladie-e-e-s and gentlemen! By the power vested in me, I give you now—the *bride and groom!*"

The guests went so wild with cheers, stomping, and hat-waving that Chris Beth found herself unable to see the honored couple.

"Speech! Speech!" the crowd roared.

"Aye, gunnies! And a speech ye'll be gettin'!"

O'Higgin? Impossible—but it was true. O'Higgin and Mrs. Malone. How could she have known? No, how could she *not* have known?

The Irishman, looking for all the world like the cat who had swallowed the canary, raised his hand for silence. "Aye, gunnies! Miss Mollie said yes, she did—and this marriage doubled me claim!"

Mrs. Malone, her usually pale gray eyes shining, took his words in stride. She extended her hand to show a wide, gold wedding band and responded. "This shows 'im to be my wedded husband and father of these children," she motioned them up front. "But," she paused dramatically, "*one* claim he'll be missin'. I'll be bearin' the name of the little ones."

Jonas, still on his perch, called out, "Rightly so! Vows last night united O'Higgin to one Mollienisia Malone, with name-rights reserved!"

"Shure and cider's a-mellowin' in the cellar—"

"O'Higgin!" His wife's eyes were stern. "Just how mellow is it?"

"Now, ye be knowin' I'm a man of moderation—not given to strong drink, Miss Mollie."

"Right, so it's coffee we'll be servin'." But there was a twinkle in her eye.

They would make a fine pair, Chris Beth knew. There was understanding born of endurance through good times and bad. There was humor and openness…. She glanced up to see Joe's eyes studying her face. It seemed only natural that the two of them should smile in understanding.

The bell rang again. The signal for dinner. More, so much more than a dinner, of course. It was Thanksgiving. And it was a wedding feast. Chris Beth felt a great surge of joy as they moved into the dining room, where the tables groaned with food.

Ordinarily the hostess would have seen that all the guests were served, but today she was the honored guest in her own house. She was to be served first, then O'Higgin, and then, wonder of wonders, the Malone children, who always had to wait for a "second table." Her friends would have it no other way.

It was all very touching to Chris Beth, and she felt a rush of tears when she saw O'Higgin hesitate at the head of the table until his beloved "Miss Mollie" nodded consent. *Praise the Lord!* There was no longer an empty chair.

32

Around the Hearth

Seated around a crackling fire in the North living room, Wilson, Joe, and the girls went over the events of the day. Nobody was hungry after the enormous dinner, so they popped corn over the open flames and drank cold cider that Wilson had stored below the waterfall by the mill. "Not too mellow for a preacher?" Joe had asked with a smile.

"Or a schoolteacher?" Chris Beth had joined in.

"Feel like I could use a lifter myself," Vangie said, stifling a little yawn. "Or don't mothers-to-be indulge?"

"Come on, you three!" Wilson objected. "That leaves just me, and you know total abstinence is my cup. Doctors are always subject to call."

"I'm going to bed!" From the way young Wil spoke up from the door, Chris Beth knew that the words were more than an announcement to his uncle. "You're leaving me out," they plainly said.

Wilson looked at the small figure, whose sullen face was half-hidden in the shadows. "Stay with us, why don't you? You know it's only cider."

The boy shook his head sullenly. "Good night, Miss Chrissy," he said and fled. Obviously, she was the only one here who counted!

Vangie was right. Young Wil resented her presence, but for a deeper reason than Chris Beth had known for sure until now. *I must talk to him,* she thought. But how did one ease the pangs of first love without breaking a young heart?

The others gave no sign of noticing. And, deep in the usual warm conversation that followed, she too forgot the incident.

Hadn't the day gone well? It had. And what a crowd! Everybody was there, even a lot of newcomers. And certainly all the old-timers. Just *everybody!*

"No," Chris Beth said slowly. "Not everybody. What about the Chu family, Wong's parents?"

"Nobody knows much about them," Wilson said, stirring the fire. "I guess nobody ever bothered to find out, actually—expected them to move on when laying of the rails stopped." He paused to lay on another backlog. Might as well. These talks always went on and on. "There was resentment among the white workers that they were here.'

"They worked for a quarter a day, you know—even used baskets and wheelbarrows. Shame. They had so much to contribute, too. They were the first to come up with black blasting powder," Joe added. "Wilson's 'magic potion.'" The two men smiled over the secret.

"Young Wil knows a few Chinese words. Maybe I—we—"

"Should call on them?" Joe finished for Chris Beth. "Yes."

"And what about the Indians?" Chris Beth paused. Maybe she was on thin ice. "Do any of them have books or Bibles?"

"Very few can speak English, let alone read," Wilson said. "Hey, I thought you Southern ladies avoided the Red Man!"

Chris Beth supposed she had stepped out of character, but an idea came to her about the upcoming Christmas program.

The crackle of the fire died down to a whisper. The four of them talked on around the embers until the room grew chilly.

Mention of the Chinese family brought up the subject of railroads. They were bound to come through, Wilson was sure. Joe was equally certain that waterways would open as planned too, allowing for steamboat trade to resume. And stagecoaches? Chris Beth had wondered, thinking of Turn-Around Inn. They would have need of a post office, and wasn't a telegrapher a nice thought, not to mention a newspaper.

The dreams spun out like cotton candy, with the four of them in the center of it all. The mill was "pulling its own weight" already (paying for itself, Chris Beth supposed), but both men wanted to get on with their studies. "We'll all be needed as growth continues," they assured the girls.

Yes, the settlement would be in need of a young doctor. Talk was that "Old Doc" was to retire as soon as Wilson could take over his practice. "Me and Gretchen's hanging up the pill bag," the aging German had said of himself and his equally-aging mare. Chris Beth wondered if Wilson had decided in favor of general practice and guessed that he had, judging by the rapt look on his face as he talked.

"And you, Joe?" Chris Beth asked when there was a lull.

"I'm glad to report that all exams are passed—written and oral," he said quietly. "I—I've waited to tell you," his eyes sought hers, "that I'll be ordained in the spring."

"Oh, that's wonderful, Joe!" Chris Beth felt a great surge of pride. "We'll all help in every way—" Her voice faltered. Maybe she was promising more than he was asking.

Wilson picked up the conversation. "Congratulations, pal! Folks need their hearts doctored as well as their bodies, I guess."

"And you ladies will be busier than ever," Joe said. "Maybe we can get a new school—" This time it was his voice that faltered. Chris Beth wondered why. Then, "and church," he added.

"And me?" Vangie spoke from beneath the pink blanket that Wilson had spread over her lap when he caught her dozing.

"*You* are going to bed, my love!" Wilson spoke the words of endearment, Chris Beth was sure, without being aware that she and Joe were in the room. But she felt no emotion, maybe because of fatigue.

The evening ended as the evenings before it had ended, as well as the many to follow—beautifully for the four of them.

The hearth of the big house seemed to be the setting for settling problems as well as for dreaming: It was there that Chris Beth finally had an opportunity for the coveted visit with Mrs. Malone (who staunchly clung to the name) and with young Wil. The men insisted that she and Vangie spend most of their time in the North living room, where (they claimed) it was warmer. And maybe it was, as they could lift bigger backlogs than she could handle alone, and she refused to let Vangie do any lifting.

Mrs. Malone rode over just before Christmas, when O'Higgin brought corn to the gristmill. O'Higgin was "fit as a fiddle," as his wife claimed. "Spoutin' off about the grizzly we saw on the way." Chris Beth could hear his brogue through the closed door as he told Wilson and Joe about the encounter. Good, that would give them a brief chat that Saturday morning.

No need to ask if things were going well. Mrs. Malone was radiant. And she knew about the children from school. Likewise, Mrs. Malone knew that the school had a floor, a new roof, and a near-wagonload of used books brought in by "educated newcomers" through the children. They had told her about the plans for the Christmas program on Christmas Eve, too. And would the four of them be coming to Turn-Around Inn for Christmas Day?

"Somethin' bothering you?" Mrs. Malone asked when Chris Beth hesitated.

"Well, yes and no. I'm concerned about what people may be thinking," she admitted.

The older woman snorted. "Who knows what they're thinkin'? It's what they're *knowin'* that counts. They know the men are upright. And given time—"

"You mean there *has* been talk? I need to know, Mrs. Malone."

"Would you look at this? Isn't it pretty like?" Mrs. Malone held out a tiny, crocheted sweater of white wool. It looked like a fairy cobweb and it was undoubtedly for Vangie. But she was not to be deterred.

Well, there were tongues that wagged anywhere, Mrs. Malone admitted. Still and all, if one went to the source—

And what was the source? Maggie, as she had suspected.

"But not to worry. She's been at Nate, but I know how to handle him. He used to come courtin' me, you know. I'll see 'im Monday. Though let's speak of you now, not others or school. You and your feelings."

"I'm fine—just—"

Mrs. Malone believed in coming right to the point. "Exceptin' in here." She patted her heart and Chris Beth nodded.

The room was silent except for the ticking of the grandfather clock. Mrs. Malone leaned forward just as O'Higgin called.

"What color are Wilson's eyes?" she asked.

"Why, I don't know," she answered, stunned. The older woman nodded. "And Joe's?"

"Hazel" she answered without hesitation. Hazel, she remembered, with little flecks of gold that showed when the light was right.

Mrs. Malone put the sweater in her bag and pulled her shawl about her. "By the way, that boy to which you was betrothed—what color eyes did he have? Thought not," she answered her own question. Later Chris Beth realized that her blank look must have admitted that she didn't remember. She hardly remembered him at all.

Sleep refused to come that night. "Vangie?" She whispered to her sister's still figure beside her. "What color are Wilson's eyes?"—

"Brown," Vangie answered. And her voice trailed away in sleep.

33

The Upper Room

Chris Beth was pleased that Joe offered to do her holiday shopping, just as he had mailed the box of holly, snowdrops, and wild grasses back. home, when he hauled excess flour and meal to the general store. There was no time to do such errands with so many demands on her time in preparation for the Christmas program. She considered including some of the cinnamon squares and sugar cookies she had baked for decorating the little tree at school when Joe mailed the package, but decided they would become stale. Besides, Mama loved winter bouquets, and the grasses and berries would be fine for that even if they were dried. She hoped her stepfather let Mama receive the package and wondered if she would understand why she and Vangie were unable to do more. She had not written to the girls.

The program was coming along. Chris Beth's main concern was where to put the spectators in case of rain. Joe suggested stretching a tarp outside and setting up the Nativity scene there, an idea she welcomed. The children were busy learning lines they had created for reenacting the first Christmas. "Why couldn't we call it that?" young Wil asked. Chris Beth was glad the other children liked the title of the play. Indeed, it was a First Christmas in so many ways. It was her and Vangie's first Christmas in the settlement, a first Christmas (*if* all went as she hoped) for truly "everybody" in the settlement to be together, a first to be expecting a real baby in her very own family, a first—well, in so many ways.

Mrs. Malone sent word by the children that she would be unable to come and "loan a hand" as planned, as she and O'Higgin were trying to finish one of the upstairs rooms for their very own. But if Chris Beth would send a list of costumes needed, she had "a-plenty old drapes for Mary, the angels, and probably the wise men." The shepherds, she said, she could outfit from O'Higgin's long woolen underwear if she didn't think they would spoil things "a-scratchin'."

"I can draw pictures of camels," young Wil said. The others volunteered for paper chains, stars, and snowflakes. Then Bertie Beltran announced that he would bring the hay. Yes, all was coming along.

As Chris Beth and young Wil worked by the hearth on the background scenery, they talked about Wong's progress. "He's reading words, Miss Chrissy, but I don't think he wants to speak pieces for the program."

Chris Beth was sure of that. "Will he come?" She wondered. She had had young Wil ask if Wong would like to have her visit his mother, and the question scared him half to death, he reported. "But they are coming on Christmas. Sort of a miracle, isn't it?" She agreed.

She had had no opportunity to speak with Boston Buck, but she had seen his one-feathered headband dart in and out of the brush and knew he was watching the preparations. Her chance would come.

Young Wil suddenly laid aside his watercolors. "Miss Chrissy," he said hesitantly, "would you like to see my tree house?"

Chris Beth was about to say yes, at some other time, but changed her mind. She needed to have a word alone with him, and it was better that he name the time and place.

The tree house was simply three boards nailed in the fork of the oak in the backyard. Over the boards the boy had stretched two burlap bags ("gunnysacks," the settlers said) for a roof. But to him it was a place of magic. "So," Chris Beth smiled, "what do you call it?"

Without hesitating, young Wil answered, "It's my Upper Room. I come here to think."

And then it all came back. Chris Beth in her playhouse. Daddy at her side. Daddy telling her stories. Chris Beth singing the little songs she had learned in Sunday school. Daddy telling her about God, "Who was so big He could love the whole world, and so small He could curl right up in each person's heart." Daddy telling her the playhouse should have a name—one fitting a need to come and be alone so she could talk things over with God. And, finally, the aching loneliness when Daddy wasn't coming home anymore...Mama's shutting herself away...and the awfulness of Daddy's empty chair...then longing for the Promised Land in her playhouse Upper Room...

Young Wil rushed to put his small arms around her. "Don't cry, Miss Chrissy—though sometimes I do here, too. I cry when I think that Uncle Wilson may marry and leave me alone again."

"Oh, darling, he'd never leave you alone. He loves you."

"But he may marry?" Young Wil paused. "May marry your sister?"

"I don't know," she said truthfully. "But if he does—"

"I'll come live with you! I want *you* to marry Uncle Wilson—or to marry both of us. I love you!"

"And I love you, too," she whispered. "But there are so many kinds of love." The child nodded and she hoped he understood.

34

A New Kind of Love

The day before Christmas dawned crystal clear. Three successive days of rain had soaked more than the earth. They had saturated Chris Beth's spirits in spite of her efforts to believe along with the children that the weather would change for the program. Then, suddenly, the clouds bumped against each other, dumped their moisture, and scurried back over the mountains for another load. Christmas Eve promised to be bright and starry-eyed.

"Then why can't we have the program outside?" Ned Malone asked. The boy was taller than she was, Chris Beth noted. The children had grown in so many ways. The others were ecstatic when Teacher said they could put it to a vote, and the "outsides" won! Actually, "Teacher" was pleased too. Beautiful night. Lantern-light reflecting shadows of the forest. Plenty of room for all. And who knew what unexpected guests might come from behind the tall fir trees?

Young Wil finished the background-mountains. Bertie scattered the hay. Up went the manger. Down went homework assignments, making room for the Christmas tree inside. Streamers. Stars. Bells. The children laughed, sang, and clapped—then stood in near-reverence. Truly, the school looked like a proper place for the Holy Birth.

Rehearsal went well, except for the giggles of "Mary" and "Joseph," a little scratching by the shepherds, and a little shoving by the "heavenly host." After a few admonitions, Chris Beth dismissed them early to go home, where the boys, she suspected, would scrub off the outer layer of skin and the girls would busy their mothers rolling their hair up on rags to create coveted curls.

"I can't believe th' crowd!" Mrs. Solomon said to Chris Beth, who was hurrying in and out just minutes before the Great Performance. "And the—uh, stage—is right nice," Nate said. He cleared his throat as if wanting to say more, but a commotion had broken out among the "cast," and she had to beg his leave and hurry inside.

"Look!" Amelia was pointing, wide-eyed, out the window. "It's Ole Tobe, and look what he brung—brought!"

By the glow of the lantern-light, Chris Beth was able to make out the dark face of "Ole Tobe," whoever he was. Who was the man and what on earth was he coaxing along? Harmony answered both questions. His wife worked for some of the "rich folks" of the settlement, "scrubbin' and things." And Ole Tobe just "kinda laid around like."

Used to be slaves, somebody thought. Long time ago—maybe a year. Never been anywhere before.

And what he led was a donkey. A real, live donkey.

Mercy! What couldn't happen on stage with "real, live" animals. Chris Beth shuddered. Then, to her relief, she saw Joe come forward, help Ole Tobe shove the balking animal near to the manger, and turn to help Wilson with a *sheep!*

Dumbfounded, she stood there even as the "littlest angel" tugged at her skirt and said, "I couldn't help it, Miss Chrissy."

Actually, what was there for her to do anyway that she hadn't done in the afternoon? she wondered later. What she would have supposed to be a finished job was in reality only the groundwork for what was taking place. Men and women were rushing about everywhere inside and outside. The Christmas tree, which recently held only her own cookies, was now looped with popcorn strands, doughnuts, and what appeared to be fortune cookies. But who ever heard *of feathers* on a Christmas tree? That could mean only one thing.

"Missy Chrissy, Missy Chrissy!" *Wong?* Why, he had never spoken to her before. But, of course, that was no greater than any of the other miracles, of the evening. Wait! What on earth was he doing taking the rag doll from the manger? She must stop him. But before she could so much as move a muscle, an Oriental man, wearing a kimono-like robe, with his dark hair twisted into a *queue,* leaned over and placed a flannel-wrapped baby carefully on the straw.

"What do you know!" Mrs. Malone, who had moved noiselessly behind her, whispered, "a livin' China baby."

Never had there been such a program in the settlement, the valley folk murmured as they helped themselves generously to the great baskets of goodies the ladies provided and drank the rich black coffee that Wilson went home to make while "Brother Joseph" read Luke's account of Christ's birth. There just never could be one like it!

Later, lying in bed far too happy to sleep, Chris Beth knew that they were right. The program had been a miracle from start to finish. Somewhere between sleep and reality, she recalled Ole Tobe's getting into the act without intending to, and the crowd's obvious delight.

"We. all dun goin' to have us a Crismas program, iffen we can get this dum' sheep in the corncrib," he announced to the audience. Then, turning to the boys and girls, he continued, "Then, *ooooh,* little child'urn, you's goin' to hear the sweetest story this side o' heben…

Well, it had been, she thought drowsily. Never had she heard the glorious Christmas message read so beautifully. How could Joe ever have doubted himself? Why, he had had the audience in his hand. Her too, when he finished with, "The birth of Jesus was more than a pretty story for children or an event to record in a history book. It gave us a whole new meaning of love." *A whole new meaning of love.*

As she drifted into a deep sleep, Chris Beth realized that it was so in her life. Here she had met people whose hearts brimmed over with Christian love. Here she had met Joe...and Wilson...and Mrs. Malone...but, most of all, she had met their God. No, not *their* God. And, no, she hadn't met Him for the first time. She had just become reacquainted with the God of her father, who loved the world...and could curl right up inside each heart...in a personal kind of way. She wanted to tell the world.

Somewhere the chimes were ringing out. It was Christmas Day. But Chris Beth slept soundly, little knowing that she had begun to tell the world already.

35

Exchange of Gifts

The good weather held—one of God's gifts for the holidays, Mrs. Malone said of Christmas Day. The air was as crisp as new cider, and the five guests (six, counting Esau) were in high spirits as they rode to Turn-Around Inn. They sang carols, trying to harmonize when their vehicles were close enough to each other. But Dobbin and Charlie Horse seemed to have sensed the mood of the riders and tried to race along the still-slippery road. Soon the road would become impassable, Joe told Chris Beth, but for now she refused to let anything mar her happiness.

Everything was perfect, or nearly so. She still wondered if Maggie would make trouble. It would have been a comfort to see her among last night's happy faces. She wondered, too, if young Wil would ever soften his stand about Wilson's obvious love for Vangie. Maybe if her sister hadn't volunteered to take the dog, he would have ridden with them today instead of with her and Joe. Well, something would turn up. So thinking, she had helped load the pile of brightly wrapped gifts which all the people had said they were *not* going to give. But wasn't that a part of the wonder of Christmas?

The atmosphere was equally festive at Turn-Around Inn. The children were wild with anticipation, and even Esau and Wolf wagged their tails at each other. After Joe read the Love Chapter in Paul's letter to the Corinthians, and there were a few moments for "silent meditatin'," O'Higgin announced, "That be meditatin' long enough!" and everybody crowded around the table, Mrs. Malone making an exception and not insisting that "company go first."

Dishes done, O'Higgin took all of them upstairs to inspect the progress on the building project. "Do you have a name for it?" young Wil asked of Mrs. Malone.

"Hadn't thought on it," she admitted.—

To Chris Beth's surprise, Vangie spoke up. "Why don't you come up with a name, Wil?"

The boy looked at her suspiciously a moment, then raised an eyebrow in question. "Well?" the older woman prompted.

Please, Lord, Chris Beth's heart whispered.

Wil allowed himself to think, of course. And then he said, "Why not call it the Upper Room?"

"Oh, *do!*" Vangie broke in. Mrs. Malone agreed. And Chris Beth let out a wee prayer of thanksgiving. Vangie had won the heart of young Wil.

In exchange of gifts that followed, it seemed to Chris Beth that each one, for its own special reason, outdid the one preceding. There was Vangie's gift of "Cozy," the white kitten she had found near the mill, to young Wil (which explained why she had insisted that Esau ride with her and Wilson, the little animal having ridden quietly in a basket without a mew!). Then there was young Wil's obvious delight (a gift in itself). Colored-yarn strings came off packages so fast that it was impossible to remember who gave what to whom.

But some of the gifts stood out. There was Wilson's little book of pressed leaves to Chris Beth, with the leaves apparently saved from their first trip through the autumn woods. *Now, don't cry,* Chris Beth warned herself. But why not? Everybody else seemed to be spilling tears all over the front-room carpet—enough to water the Christmas tree!

Mrs. Malone was crying over a big, red, heart-shaped box from O'Higgin. No wonder! It was the box she had handled so longingly at the general store. The Malone girls were not crying exactly, but their eyes looked suspiciously bright as one by one they unfolded their spanking-new dresses of bright calico. The way Joe opened the small copy of the New Testament that Chris Beth had ordered from the catalog made her wonder if he too would cry. Instead, he squeezed her hand. She felt the color rise to her cheeks. Maybe she should remove her hand. But she didn't.

Emotions reached their peak when, after a scramble of mittens, mufflers, and "pound cakes all around," Vangie presented an intricate piece of needlepoint to Mrs. Malone, saying it was for the Upper Room. Mrs. Malone, trying to get "my silly self under control," brought an entire layette for the new baby! It was Vangie's turn to cry—and O'Higgin's when he opened the package from Mrs. Malone. "Begory!" whooped the big Irishman at sight of the braided whip. "Not that he'll use it and not like I could afford it either, but it's not right his covetin' it since seem the like when Mr. President passed through."

The timing was just right. Chris Beth handed a plain envelope to Mrs. Malone. "For the two of you," she said. And there inside were probably more dollar bills than they had ever seen at a single viewing.

"I will not take this," Mrs. Malone said stoutly. "You was my guest, not my boarder!"

"And this is my gift, not my payment."

Instead of further objecting, Mrs. Malone blew her nose, and led Chris Beth to the corner where sat a hand-finished chest. "Made it in his spare time." She nodded to a beaming O'Higgin.

"Oh, Mrs. Malone, it's *beautiful!*"

"Open it, then."

Chris Beth stared in astonishment at the stacks of bleached flour sacks, all snowy-white and embroidered with everything from wild flowers to teapots—each bearing the initials C.E.K.

"Now there will be no more foolish tears," Mrs. Malone said matter-of-factly. "It's time for mince pie and coffee before the sun sets. Oh," she called over her shoulder, "them's for your hope chest!" No crying, Mrs. Malone had said, but how about blushing?

One couldn't gild a lily, Chris Beth had always heard. Well, Joe and Wilson could! As the five of them sat toasting their toes by the fire back at the North house, Joe spoke to Wilson, "Me first?"

At Wilson's nod, Joe removed a velvet box from his pocket, opened it unceremoniously, and removed a dainty gold lavaliere. "My mother's," he said simply. "Will you wear it, Chris Beth?"

"With pride," she said with equal simplicity.

Young Wil left his new books, notebook for leaf collections, and tool chest to watch as Joe fastened the chain around Chris Beth's throat. Did he intend to say something? Apparently not. The boy went back to his gifts and Wilson, ill-at-ease for the first time Chris Beth remembered, tried to untie the ribbon on a small box—obviously a gift for Vangie.

"Here, let me do it," young Wil said with the special impatience that children reserve for adults. His uncle handed him the box.

Vangie gasped, "Oh, Wilson!" when she saw the ring with a pearl mounted in the quaint style of his mother's generation. Without another word, she extended her left hand and he slipped the ring on it carefully. The lavaliere had been a surprise. The ring was not, it was plain to see. Suddenly everybody seemed to be embracing everybody else on this wonderful day which had held so many surprises and emotions. This was so right for Vangie, Chris Beth realized. She herself had long since put away any feelings she might have had to the contrary. As she had told young Wil, where was he? To her relief, he was still with his gifts, though it was plain to see that he was not concentrating.

"Yoo hoo! Congratulations are in order," she called to him.

"Want to be first to kiss the bride-to-be?" Wilson smiled.

Young Wil studied his shoes. "Kissing's silly."

"Often is," Vangie surprised Chris Beth by agreeing, "but how about a handshake?" She watched as young Wil complied—proud of them both, and a lot in love with everybody in the room!

36

Flood!

The weeks went tumbling end on end, and suddenly it was February. Although the mountains were robed in snow, the valley put on its green girdle of spring. The meadows, kept growing all winter by the rain, were embroidered here and there with sleepy buttercups. O'Higgin pointed to the heavy catkin-wigs that the walnut trees wore and predicted the best crop ever. Chris Beth filled the classroom with fat pussy willows. Mrs. Malone let the early baby chicks out for occasional days when sun and showers played tag, but kept a "weather eye" out. "It's a false spring we're gettin'," she said darkly. Chris Beth and Vangie smiled indulgently, ignoring the older woman's warning that "nobody predicts Oregon weather but fools and newcomers." The worst was over.

The roads had been so bad at times that the wagon wheels mired to the hubs. The valley folk had almost everything they needed, having looked ahead, and what they lacked some friendly neighbor supplied. But there was a need for Brother Jonas to make one of his seldom visits. Nobody felt the need more keenly than Wilson and Vangie. Vangie, Chris Beth noted, had blossomed. Approaching motherhood became her. Under Wilson's watchful eye, things had gone well in spite of her fragility. But it was easy to understand her decision to yield to Wilson's insistence that they be married before the baby's arrival. Not that neighbors doubted her widowhood (Maggie's attempt at gossip had been more about the living arrangement the four of them had settled upon). The real reason for wanting the wedding before April was that Wilson wanted to make the baby a "true North."

As Vangie sewed the doll-like garments which the new arrival would need and Chris Beth worked long hours on lesson plans that she hoped would meet the needs of her at-all-levels students, the sisters laughed a lot as they wondered which would arrive first—the stork or the circuit rider. "Wouldn't we shock Mama right off her day-bed?" Vangie giggled. "First we're wayward, then we're liberal!"

Mama's package (slipped out by her one remaining servant, she had said) came after the holidays. It had silk (for making a long christening gown, she said). Instead, Vangie used it to line a padded "receiving box" which she could transport in the buggy. She and the baby would be making house calls with Wilson, she said proudly. Mama had sent velvet for drapes, too. It was totally inappropriate for a log cabin, the girls admitted, but one of these days, who knew?

Some of the work slacked off at the mill, which gave both Joe and Wilson time for further preparation for their professions. Wilson was to take over Doc's practice in late spring, having put in more time than internship required when the bad epidemic of measles broke out. "Someday," he said, "there will be no need for losing children with complications resulting from childhood diseases." That hope, Chris Beth knew, was his reason for pursuing pathology as time allowed.

Joe was looking a little tired. Mrs. Malone said it was "his liver," and Chris Beth wondered if he ate right when she wasn't around. Wilson assured them both that it was neither. He was studying too hard. "Not afraid he won't make it, but to him it makes a differ-ence how *well.*" Yes, Chris Beth knew, Joe was like that—a totally dedicated man. Occasionally she let her mind wonder foolishly just what being a minister's wife would be like. Surely nobody in her right mind would consider the role! Once, talking about "somebody else," of course, she had said that most women would feel unworthy.

Joe's smile looked a little crooked somehow. "Most ministers feel so, too. I—I'm not exactly preparing for my final exam for the saint-hood myself."

But don't let the little doubts keep you from the pulpit, her heart pleaded. Still, she felt she had no right to speak out. Inwardly she hoped that something would prove to this wonderful man just how right he was for the ministry.

There was to be a taffy-pull at the general store the night the flood came. *Would people really travel that far?* Chris Beth wondered. They would. *In spite of the rain?* Yes, unless the creeks were rising—and certainly the February break had helped dry out the roads. Well, it made little difference to the four of them. They had said polite "No's" to pie socials, quilting bees, and even the "Big Stomp," when (for good luck) it was customary for the entire population to turn out. The purpose was to smooth the newly laid floor as children played and adults square-danced away the night. It was unwise for Vangie, Wilson said. Yes, and all of them were busy. As a matter of fact, Chris Beth made certain that O'Higgin and Mrs. Malone were along when the four appeared anywhere together. Maybe Maggie would have less of a case if they were properly chaperoned. One day they would have to reckon with what they were doing, she supposed. Vangie and Wilson would "make things right," but—she always stopped her thinking at that point. She would just have to find a place when Joe moved back into the cabin...

Clouds began building up early in the day of the taffy-pull. They were innocent-looking enough at first but later built into white towers edged in darkness. "Back home I'd think we were to have a real blow," she told the children. Looking again, she felt an uneasiness growing inside. "Since it's the night of the party at the Solomons, why don't we dismiss early?"

The youngsters romped through the door and disappeared in their separate directions, whooping with the joy of school-let-out. Then there was an eerie silence. Maybe she should, go home too. Even as she reached the decision, she was aware of great puffs of wind. Thinking it would be cold outside, she secured her cape about herself.

Outside, however, it was warm—too warm. Why, the wind was almost hot! Even so, its force was terrible. Bracing herself against it, she rushed toward the footbridge. A heavy tattoo of great raindrops nearly swept her off her feet. The sky was black now, and it was hard to see. Her cape was wrenched from her hands as the rain came down in torrents. Her hair fell in wet, tangled disarray and her long skirt—drenched through and through—clung to her boots, threatening to trip her every step. "Joe! Joe!" she screamed wildly against the roar of the storm. Behind her there was a splintering crash. The school? No, the graveyard shack! Then she knew she had become disoriented and had traveled in the wrong direction. She was near the cemetery, on flat ground, near the creek on the opposite side. Water was roaring through the creek, but how could it all happen so fast? She had no way of knowing, of course, that the Chinook winds—fear of the settlers—had come too early, melting the snowpack and causing streams and rivers to rise, breaking the feeble dam the men had built in hopes of staving off such disasters. She only knew that the earth trembled.

Somewhere back of her a light flashed. Lightning? Where *was* everybody? Vangie would be scared…water was rising around her boots…she couldn't move…the light of a lantern exploded in her face, blinding her, and she was lifted in a pair of gentle arms…

When Chris Beth became aware of what was going on about her, she realized that she was in a strange room. But the face above her was dearly familiar. "Joe, *Joe—*" she whispered. Then his had been the arms!

"Thank God," he whispered against her wet hair, which had fallen hopelessly around her shoulders. But before there was time for further conversation, a familiar voice said from the doorway, "Joe!" She recognized it as belonging to Mrs. Malone. She looked around her. Of course! She was in the Upper Room of the Turn-Around Inn. But where was all the noise coming from? What had happened?

As she began to recall the events, Chris Beth knew that by some miracle Joe had come for her. But now others were in need. She could hear sobbing and screams from below. Hurriedly, stumbling at first, then more sure of herself, she wrapped her head in a towel from the washstand and hurried to the top of the stairs. Joe would be needing her, as would Wilson, Vangie, and all the others! For, to her great joy, she had spotted them all below—even young Wil, who was helping his uncle lay the writhing body of a young woman on a stretcher improvised from a quilt. And *Vangie!* Vangie was standing on the other side, rubbing the woman's wrists and speaking in the professional tones of a much-concerned nurse.

The group moved into a downstairs room, but not before Chris Beth recognized the young Mrs. Martin, who was about to give birth to her child. She sent up a little prayer and motioned for Joe to help some of the people upstairs, who appeared uninjured but were sobbing in the way that told her they had suffered losses too great to bear. She met him halfway, offering words of encouragement.

After that she lost all track of time. In one sense it seemed to drag through eternity while in another it was all over in the twinkling of an eye. How many times, she wondered later, did she and Joe travel wordlessly downstairs and up again? How many people did they comfort? She only heard enough to know that homes were gone, people were missing, livestock was swept downstream before there was time to get them to higher ground, and that young Mrs. Martin wasn't going to make it. Her husband had been drowned in trying to get to Doc Dagan, but the baby boy, maybe, would live.

It was unreal. It was a bad dream. It would go away. Nothing would come into focus except Joe's dear face as his great eyes met hers over the huddled forms of those bereaved.

The long gray fingers of an ugly dawn were poking at the windows. The world outside was sodden. But inside all was quiet—temporarily. Sometime during the "awful glory" of the night, Joe had leaned over one of the sleeping guests and whispered, "Will you marry me?" And she, too weary to speak, had nodded, "Yes." Then, with hands clasped across the bed, they had fallen into an exhausted slumber.

There Mrs. Malone found them when she took a head count and brought in great mugs of steaming coffee. It was still raining, she told them. In spite of that, the water was receding because the snowpack had melted. "It was like the end of the world," Mrs. Malone said of the storm. "An awful boom, then without warning the big wall of water. Lots of folks on their way to the general store got stranded, as you see—just God's blessing they was near." She paused just as her husband brought still-hot sourdough biscuits with butter oozing tantalizingly down their sides. "Eat up, both o' ye. 'Twas like the demons o' hell, that wind! Took down our peach trees and blew away the chicken coops."

Between the two of them they told of the death and destruction which the now-receding river and the big blow had left behind. "But the good Lord always brings good from adversity," Mrs. Malone summed up the tragedy. "Land that was swept away's replaced, I wager, with rich silt from the riverbed. Things'll green up for sure now. And here in the settlement, miracles are goin' on." Her knowing eyes told Chris Beth that she and Joe were one of them, and then she went on, "Dare say one took place in the downstairs side room where poor little Miz Martin died—givin' us a chance to rally round—"

"*Died!*" Joe sprang up, but O'Higgin restrained him. "Your job not be finished here—or Wilson's—that be why we have ye sleepin'. Jonas showed, he did, and he took care of the needs."

"Put her away real nice," Mrs. Malone added. "Poor little thing died never knowin' her husband's body's now on its way to the ocean to be buried at sea, or that their cabin in the lowlands went with him. But," she brightened, "she rallied long enough for Wilson and Vangie to let 'er know the baby's alive—very much so. Lustiest lungs I've known for a spell. Well, best we get downstairs, O'Higgin. Others need feedin'."

"I'll go with you," Chris Beth said quickly. "I need to wash up." She needed time to think, too. Had Joe really proposed?

As she washed in the basin by the pump, Chris Beth wondered if some of what happened in the Upper Room could have been a dream. Would Joe—quiet, unassuming, and shy though he was—take so great a step in such circumstances? Wouldn't he choose a more appropriate time and place? The cold water on her face and the bracing coffee did their job. She was wide awake—and wildly exhilarated. Of course he would! What better setting than as the two of them did the job the Lord had chosen them for in the first place?

She tiptoed back upstairs. There were things they needed to talk about. The circuit rider would be here a while, as was his habit, to stay "bindin' up wounds." There was the matter of the contract, of course. Well, she would let Joe come up with some solutions.

But he had no opportunity. Mrs. Malone, having witnessed so many miracles during the last 24 hours, seemed in need of one more. Soundlessly she tiptoed up behind Chris Beth with the newborn Baby Martin in her arms. "Well, which of you wants him?" Chris Beth and Joe both reached out, joining hands as they did so. It was all too wonderfully incredible to be believed, even by the settlers who had gathered below. Prayer was a powerful instrument, but this time the Lord's answer left them astounded. *Brother Joseph was sliding down the banister!*

37

Double Wedding—Triple Joy

It was a beautiful wedding. Valley folks talked about it for years. Like the Christmas program, they said, there had never been anything like it in the settlement, and most likely they would never see another one so grand.

Of course, it was a "mite peculiar," what with one bride ready "to deliver" and the other with a week-old baby! All understandable, though, since the one ready for "her confinement" was widowed and the other had taken in the orphan child. Nice that he'd be "wearin' the family name of the other parents—probably call him 'Mart.'" A little unusual that a woman Mollie Malone's age would be a bridesmaid—well, matron-of-honor—but circumstances warranted it, considering that somebody had to hold the Martin baby and everybody knew that young teacher refused to let him out of her sight. Lucky child, they all agreed.

Didn't young Wil look handsome standing up there like a little man, handing out rings all around? First double-best man they'd ever seen. Maybe that's the way folks did things down South or back East, "'specially when it's double kin," what with Miss Chrissy marrying Brother Joseph and her younger sister marrying young Dr. North. Why, the boys were like brothers!

O'Higgin looked like he had just licked the cream off Mollie's churning! Likely the only reason he got to do the honors of giving

Miss Evangeline away was to keep him from those croupy things he called bagpipes! But one thing there was simply no explaining. How in the world did Nate Goldsmith get hog-tied into giving their beloved teacher away? He had vowed all over the neighborhood that contracts were binding come "you-know-what and high water." Of course, some said the president of the board got himself a bit of both! Seems Mollie and Olga descended on him at the same time. *Olga?* His "ole woman"!

Wilson North would be a fine doctor. He was bound to prosper with all he had going on, and folks were sure to get sick even with home remedies. But Brother Joseph? He was a "called preacher" all right, but wouldn't a church be out of the question after all the damages of the flood? Well, they'd all pitch in and help. It was customary to "pound the preacher," and they sure had everything to do it with—all the dried fruit, smoked hams, and canned goods. And Bertie Solomon had talked about their need for staples. Depend on Bertie to come through in time of trouble!

Chris Beth and Vangie waited beside the fireplace-setting of the improvised altar. How good of Mrs. Malone to have thought of it, but, then, how good of her to have taken over the entire wedding completely as she did. It would have been unwise for Vangie to try to descend the stairs, lovely though it might have been. Chris Beth tucked in the corners of her mouth lest she smile when the grooms came down instead. Mrs. Malone had declared herself "bound and determined" that somebody was coming out of the Upper Room. What would these wonderful people think if Joe decided to *slide* down to meet her?

What the audience saw was Miss Chrissy, "a vision in white wearing Miss Mollie's wedding dress," as she looked demurely at her bouquet. Little did they know (Chris Beth hoped!) that it was hard to erase the memory of Joe's wild trip down those banisters when she had said "Yes" to his proposal and to their taking the baby just as readily. One look at her lovely bouquet—lilies of the valley and early daffodils from Mrs. Malone's "protected side of the house," plus the leaves Joe had so thoughtfully preserved—eased the urge to smile and brought the urge to weep with tenderness. Never would she forget the beauty of their first day in the autumn woods. That was the day the two of them had expressed their "hidden desires"— hers to tramp through the autumn leaves and his to slide down the banisters at Turn-Around Inn. Surely God had fulfilled each desire, hidden or unknown to them.

Vangie's nosegay of violets (to match Mrs. Malone's blue crepe "second-day dress" she had so thoughtfully altered for her) trembled, but Vangie's smile was reassuring as their eyes met across their bouquets.

I guess I'll always feel a need to protect her, Chris Beth thought. But, mixed with the tenderness and concern, she felt a growing admiration for her sister. Why, the two of them were true "pioneer women" now—maybe possessing, if the truth were known, more courage than most. After all, other women their ages who had braved the challenges of the frontier had men at their sides—husbands or fathers. They— two frightened, gently bred girls—had come alone. And made it!

Somewhere there were the faint but unmistakable strains of *Lohengrin*. The Goldsmiths had brought the old organ to Turn-Around Inn at the height of last week's storm, when it looked as if the floodwaters might take their cabin. "Might as well leave it for services. Planned on donatin' it to the new church anyway," Nate had decided. "Old woman plays fer funerals and weddin's—glad it's the latter this day!" It could have been the other way, his voice implied, as he apparently recalled the battle over the broken terms of his sacred contract.

Somebody in the audience began to hum the wedding march along with the organ. And then the crowd joined in.

Yes! It was a beautiful wedding, but Chris Beth was unaware. She only knew that Joe, wonderful Joe, was coming down the stairs and that his eyes, never leaving her face, sparkled with tiny flecks of gold...

38

Bless This House!

Later, as the ladies of the settlement opened their bulging baskets to lay out the wedding feast, Chris Beth placed the sleeping baby in his father's arms. "Joe, try and understand. I need just a minute with Vangie." Of course he understood, Joe's eyes said as proudly their gaze met over the tiny form of their first son. The baby inhaled deeply, then settled back into the fleecy, pink-cloud blanket shared from Vangie's layette.

"Joe—" She wanted to tell her husband that everything was going to be all right. One day they would have their church. God had brought them together for His purpose, and He would see to it that His purpose was served.

And there was so much else she wanted to say about this love they shared, for it was very special. Beginning in friendship, love was the gentle stranger that moved in silently—and then caught fire. It understood and shared and forgave through good times and bad. It did not, as the Bible said, "seek its own way," but allowed for human frailties. And when a woman had the love of a good man, a family, and a circle of loyal friends, she was rich! Without it, though she gain the whole world, it would never be enough. Money could not purchase liberty, life—or love!

"Chris Beth—Chrissy darling, what is it?" Joe looked at her with concern.

The eloquent words would not come, of course. Love such as she offered could only spell itself out in the heart-to-heart living from, this day forward—hoping all things for the future and forgetting all things that were past. No longer did she wish time to stand still. Love must blaze new trails, riding over petty irritations and big problems, the little heartbreaks and the great sorrows, into the bright new tomorrow—together.

Instead, she said, "Nothing. It's just—just that I love you so much!" Then, as tears streamed down her face, she shooed him away as he would take her into his arms and motioned Vangie into the side room where she and Wilson had brought little Mart into the world.

Vangie, still clutching her violets, walked in. As the two couples went their separate ways later, they just had to toss out their bouquets together, Mrs. Malone insisted. They owed her that.

"Are you all right, Chrissy?" Vangie asked. Thoughtfulness was new to her, and Chris Beth's heart warmed even more at how it became her.

She nodded and reached into the bag she had packed for little Mart's use while she and Joe had a few days alone at the cabin. "Come closer," she said, pulling a small satin box from among the receiving blankets and hand-hemmed dresses. From it she lifted the exquisite pearl-and-sapphire brooch that Vangie had never seen.

Vangie gasped. "What—where?" She begged an explanation.

"'Something blue,'" she said. "I couldn't bring myself to look at it again until after your wedding." She held up a restraining hand when Vangie would have spoken. "Someday maybe, but not now, Vangie. Just wear it for me. Please do. Turn it into a beautiful memory instead of the nightmare it has been."

Vangie, still puzzled, obliged. She tried very hard to pin the brooch at the high neckline of her blue "second day" dress. "Here, let me," Chris Beth said when Vangie fumbled. The brooch, once a hateful reminder, nestled among the ruffles of the crepe gown as if it had always belonged there. If pearls were for tears, as Mama always said, they had been shed quite enough, Chris Beth knew. The blue of the sparkling sapphire matched the Oregon sky outside, where a few soft cumulous clouds promised fair weather ahead. Not a trace of gloom remained in her heart.

The two sisters embraced wordlessly. No words could express their emotions. And sometimes, both of them knew, silence was better.

About the Author

June Masters Bacher (1918–1993) was a beloved teacher, news reporter, scriptwriter, and prolific author. Her many pioneer romance novels have sold well over a million copies. She also published inspirational magazine articles, devotionals, a collection of poems, and cookbooks.

More Great Inspirational Romance
Novels from Sweet River Press

June Masters Bacher's pioneer romance stories

Love's Soft Whisper
Sent away from family and friends, young Courtney Glamora begins a long, mysterious journey to find adventure, love, and faith in the rugged Columbia Territory.

Love's Beautiful Dream
A beautiful spring in the Columbia Valley provides the perfect scene for Courtney and Clint to prepare for their upcoming wedding. But a terrible accident and some unwelcome guests prompt Courtney to risk her life for love.

MaryAnn Minatra's Alcott Legacy series

The Tapestry
From Tenessee battlefields to the White House itself, this sweeping Civil War epic traces the lives of two brothers—linked only by a broken locket—the people who loved them, and the triumph of faithful prayer.

The Masterpiece
One man fought for the Blue, the other, the Gray. But not even the Civil War could divide the Alcott family.

The Heirloom
Fifty years earlier, Ben Alcott's grandfather wore Union blue in the War Between the States. Now Ben is engaged in another fight for freedom—this time on European soil.

Wonderful Inspirational Romance Novels from Harvest House Publishers

BIG SKY DREAMS SERIES
by Lori Wick

Cassidy

Cassidy Norton makes her living sewing for others, and her life is full. Still, Cassidy wants a family, but that would mean revealing the details of her life before Token Creek. Will she find the strength to take that risk?

Sabrina

Sabrina Matthews, a young prostitute in frontier Denver, comes to Christ and moves to Token Creek, where she finds herself falling for Pastor Rylan Jarvik. A moving novel about past mistakes and forgiveness.

Jessie

Book three in bestselling author Lori Wick's popular Big Sky Dreams series transports you to the Montana Territory in the late 1800s where you meet Jessie Wheeler, whose long-absent husband, Seth, returns to prove his love. But can Jessie trust him or God with her family's future?

BJ HOFF

American Anthem

This thrilling saga, set in 1870's New York, transports you into another time to share the hopes and dreams and triumphant faith of a people you'll grow to love...and never forget.

To learn more about these books, read sample chapters, or find more great Harvest House books, log on to our website:

www.harvesthousepublishers.com

HARVEST HOUSE
PUBLISHERS